The Vampire
Lord Ruthwen

also by Brian Stableford:
The Empire of the Necromancers (1: The Shadow of Frankenstein; 2: Frankenstein and the Vampire Countess; 3: Frankenstein in London); The New Faust at the Tragicomique; Sherlock Holmes and the Vampires of Eternity; The Stones of Camelot; The Wayward Muse.

also translated and introduced by Brian Stableford:
Anonymous: Sâr Dubnotal vs. Jack the Ripper; *Anthologies*: News from the Moon; The Germans on Venus; The Supreme Progress; *Cyprien Bérard*: The Vampire Lord Ruthwen; *Richard Bessière*: The Gardens of the Apocalypse; *Félix Bodin*: The Novel of the Future; *André Caroff*: The Terror of Madame Atomos; *Charles Derennes*: The People of the Pole; *Henri Duvernois*: The Man Who Found Himself; *Achille Eyraud*: Voyage to Venus; *Henri Falk*: The Age of Lead; *Paul Féval*: Anne of the Isles; The Black Coats (1: 'Salem Street; 2: The Invisible Weapon; 3: The Parisian Jungle; 4: The Companions of the Treasure; 5: Heart of Steel; 6: The Cadet Gang); John Devil; Knightshade; Revenants; Vampire City; The Vampire Countess; The Wandering Jew's Daughter; *Paul Féval, fils*: Felifax, the Tiger-Man; *Octave Joncquel & Théo Varlet*: The Martian Epic; *Jean de La Hire*: The Nyctalope vs. Lucifer; The Nyctalope on Mars; Enter the Nyctalope; *Georges Le Faure & Henri de Graffigny*: The Extraordinary Adventures of a Russian Scientist Across the Solar System (2 vols.); *Gustave Le Rouge*: The Vampires of Mars; *Jules Lermina*: Panic in Paris; Mysteryville; The Secret of Zippelius; *Marie Nizet*: Captain Vampire; *Henri de Parville*: An Inhabitant of the Planet Mars; *Gaston de Pawlowski*: Journey to the Land of the 4th Dimension; *P.-A. Ponson du Terrail*: The Vampire and the Devil's Son; *Maurice Renard*: The Blue Peril; Doctor Lerne; The Doctored Man; A Man Among the Microbes; The Master of Light; *Albert Robida*: The Clock of the Centuries; The Adventures of Saturnin Farandoul; Chalet in the Sky; *J.-H. Rosny Aîné*: The Givreuse Enigma; The Mysterious Force; The Navigators of Space; Vamireh; The World of the Variants; The Young Vampire; *Han Ryner*: The Superhumans; *Jacques Spitz:* The Eye of Purgatory; *Kurt Steiner*: Ortog; *Villiers de l'Isle-Adam*: The Scaffold; The Vampire Soul; *Philippe Ward & S. Miller*: The Song of Montségur.

The Vampire
Lord Ruthwen

by
Cyprien Bérard

translated by
Brian Stableford

A Black Coat Press Book

Visit our website at www.blackcoatpress.com

ISBN 978-1-61227-004-3. First Printing. April 2011. Published by Black Coat Press, an imprint of Hollywood Comics.com, LLC, P.O. Box 17270, Encino, CA 91416. All rights reserved. Except for review purposes, no part of this book may be reproduced or transmitted in any form or by any means, electronic or mechanical, including photocopying, recording, or by any information storage and retrieval system, without permission in writing from the publisher. The stories and characters depicted in this novel are entirely fictional. Printed in the United States of America.

TABLE OF CONTENTS

Publisher's Note

This is the fourth volume dedicated to the character of Lord Ruthven (or, in this case, "Ruthwen") published by Black Coat Press, the other three being:

• *Lord Ruthven the Vampyre* (ISBN 9781932983104), which includes the original 1819 novelette by John William Polidori, which started it all; two extracts of letters from Polidori; a fragment from an uncompleted novel by Lord Byron showing his own take on the character; an 1820 stage play by Charles Nodier (with possible uncredited assistance by Achille de Jouffroy, Jean Toussaint Merle and Carmouche), *Le Vampire*, translated by Frank J. Morlock as *The Vampire*; an 1821 vaudeville play by Eugène Scribe and Mélesville also entitled *Le Vampire*, translated by Morlock as *Being Lord Ruthven*; and, finally, *The Adventure of the Beneficent Vampire*, an all-new story by Morlock.

• *The Return of Lord Ruthven* (ISBN 9781932983111), which includes an 1851 stage play by Alexandre Dumas, *Le Vampire*, translated by Frank J. Morlock as *The Return of Lord Ruthven*; and *Entretien with a Vampire*, an all-new story by Morlock.

• *Lord Ruthven Begins* (ISBN 9781935558439), which includes an 1865 stage play by Jules Dornay, *Douglas le Vampire*, adapted and retold by Frank J. Morlock as *Lord Ruthven Begins*; and *The Confession of Mary Queen of Scots Regarding Lord Ruthven*, an all-new story by Morlock, purporting to tell the origins of Ruthven.

Introduction

Lord Ruthwen, ou les Vampires, here translated by Brian Stableford as *The Vampire Lord Ruthwen*, was published in Paris by Ladvocat, one of the stallholders in the Palais-Royal, in 1820. It was an obvious attempt to cash in on the widespread popularity of the novelette *The Vampyre*, first published anonymously in the April 1819 issue of *The New Monthly Magazine* and rapidly reprinted, also anonymously, by Sherwood, Neely & Jones. A rumor had quickly spread that *The Vampyre* was the work of Lord Byron, and Henry Colburn soon issued a pirated version of the booklet bearing Byron's by-line, which helped domestic sales considerably. A French translation by Henry Faber, credited to Byron, was issued before the year was out by Chaumerot *jeune*. That translation was reprinted in a set of Byron's *Oeuvres complètes* published by Ladvocat in 1820, given pride of place in volume one, alongside *Le Corsaire* [The Corsair].

Byron hastened to deny that *The Vampyre* was his work, and the true author of the story was rapidly revealed to be Byron's one-time friend John William Polidori, with whom he had fallen out. Whether Ladvocat knew that when he included the translation in his *Oeuvres complètes* is unclear, but he certainly knew it by the time the sequel he had commissioned was delivered, as the fact is acknowledged in the notes thereto.

No one who has read Honoré de Balzac's *Illusions perdues*—the second part of which includes an elaborately embittered account of the exploitative and piratical working practices of the Palais-Royal book-dealers during the relevant period—would be surprised by his attempt to cash in regardless.

The confusion originated because Polidori had been present at the Villa Diodati on Lake Geneva, on an evening when he, Lord Byron, Percy Shelley, Mary Shelley and her half-sister, Claire Clairmont, each agreed to attempt to write a ghost story after sampling a recent anthology of such works. None of them completed a story at the time, but Mary Shelley made the evening famous when she credited the seed of her novel *Frankenstein; or, The Modern Prometheus* (1818) to a nightmare she had that night. Byron had, however, written a fragment of a story,[1] which he eventually published, in order to demonstrate the extent to which it differed from Polidori's story—which, once he was revealed as its author, Polidori claimed to have based on Byron's fragment (a claim reproduced in the notes to *Lord Ruthwen*).

Given these tangled circumstances, it is not particularly surprising that *Lord Ruthwen* was also deliberately misattributed by its publisher, credited to "l'auteur de *Jean Sbogar* et de *Thérèse Aubert*." Those two novels, published in 1818 and 1819 respectively (the latter by Ladvocat), were the work of the great pioneer of French Romanticism, Charles Nodier—who, it eventually transpired, had only written the "preliminary observations" to *Lord Ruthwen*, the actual text having been supplied by Cyprien Bérard. It was not the only work dealing with vampires that was misattributed to Nodier, whose name is associated to this day with a collection of supernatural anecdotes published in 1822 as *Infernaliana*, although it

---

[1] Included in *Lord Ruthen the Vampyre*, q.v.

is unlikely that he wrote any of the pieces collected therein.

Little seems to be known about Cyprien Bérard, except that he was the director of the Théâtre Vaudeville and that he founded a royalist journal, *La Foudre* [The Thunderbolt], in collaboration with the prolific playwright Marie-Emmanuel Théaulon de Lambert and Théaulon's frequent collaborator, Armand Dartois. The only other publication signed with Bérard's name is an 1825 pamphlet analyzing innovations in performance at his theater, but he had almost certainly done hackwork for Ladvocat, and had probably tried to persuade Ladvocat to publish some of his poetry and short fiction. (If the implication of the notes in *Lord Ruthwen* can be trusted, Bérard had made a translation of *The Corsair*, which have been might be the one used by Ladvocat in the *Oeuvres complètes*.)

Nodier certainly worked for Ladvocat as a translator—he was acknowledged as the translator of Charles Maturin's Gothic novel *Bertram* in 1821—and it would be perfectly in accordance with the practices described by Balzac, if he had also done unacknowledged hackwork of that sort for Ladvocat, including unauthorized translations of Byron. Nodier was also acquainted with Théaulon de Lambert (who adapted his novella *Trilby*, first published by Lavocat in 1822, for the stage), and may well have contributed to *La Foudre*. At any rate, a conspiracy of sorts was formed, and the doubly-deceptive *Lord Ruthwen* was the result.

It is difficult to believe that Nodier was able to pluck up any enthusiasm for Bérard's work, if he actually bothered to read it before praising it in his introduction—which is otherwise a straightforward apology for Romanticism, repeating arguments that he had used elsewhere and exemplified in his own works with much greater success than in Bérard's, but he was certainly sincere in his advocacy of new directions in French literature. It is significant, however, that in spite of its misattribution, *Lord Ruthwen* was never reprinted.

The protagonist of the original novelette *The Vampyre* is a naive "young gentleman" named Aubrey, an orphan who shares his vast inheritance with his sister. Recently arrived in London society, he encounters the charismatic Lord Ruthven (*sic*), who invites him to join him on a continental tour that he is about to make—apparently in order to flee his creditors. The two eventually separate in Rome, where Aubrey's growing suspicions regarding Ruthven's bad character are confirmed by letters from home. Before leaving Italy for Greece, Aubrey frustrates one of Ruthven's schemes, whose target is an intended bride.

In Greece, Aubrey encounters a beautiful girl named Ianthe, who quickly falls victim to a "vampire," and falls ill himself thereafter. He is, however, found and cared for by a seemingly-repentant Ruthven. Ruthven is then shot by bandits, and while he is apparently on his deathbed, he exacts a promise from Aubrey that the younger man will never say anything to compromise his reputation. When he eventually returns home, haunted by apparitions of Ruthven, Aubrey falls seriously ill again. This time, he is cared for by his sister, until she becomes engaged to be married. He is told that her fiancé is the Earl of Marsden, but finds out as the marriage is taking place that Marsden and Ruthven are one and the same. He finally breaks his oath, but he is too late—the last line of the story reveals that his sister has already "glutted the thirst of a VAMPYRE!"

The events of the story are usually read as a sly transfiguration of Polidori's own relationship with Byron, who took him to the continent when it was politic for him to leave England, ostensibly to serve as his private physician. The two quarreled continually, allegedly as a result of Polidori's bitter envy of his benefactor's wealth and talent; Polidori was dismissed in the summer of 1816, although Byron had to get him out of trouble in Milan thereafter, and apparently tried to fix up various appointments for him.

Polidori was undoubtedly familiar with the scurrilous Gothic *roman à clef* by means of which the scorned and furious Lady Caroline Lamb had attempted to pay Byron back for rejecting her, *Glenarvon* (1816), and it is obviously no coincidence that the name of Polidori's villain echoes that of Lady Caroline Lamb's protagonist, Ruthven Glenarvon. Exactly how much malice there was in Polidori's transfiguration is, however, open to doubt, given that he really does seem to have been a remarkably naïve and unselfconscious young man. It is equally dubious, however, that he really was surprised as he claimed to be when *The Vampyre* was published—a circumstance for which he disclaimed all responsibility.

Poor Polidori, alas, never had the chance to appreciate what he had wrought; he was knocked down in a traffic accident and suffered brain damage, suffering a long dementia before dying on August 27, 1821, at the age of 25. He was survived by two sisters, one of whom muddied the waters further by carefully obliterating all the passages in his diary relating to Lord Byron, apparently for prudish reasons, thus preventing further research into his apparent grievances. (His other sister became the mother of Dante Gabriel Rossetti and Christina Rossetti.) He died presuming that he would never get credit for *The Vampyre*, having carelessly and unjustly lost that credit to his *bête noire*, but Byron was very enthusiastic to return it to him, and eventually succeeded in doing so, although the poet was unable to prevent its supplementation of his own image with an extra measure of the sinister.

Although his contribution to *Lord Ruthwen* was minimal, Charles Nodier did make some contribution, in collaboration with Achille de Jouffroy and the director of the Théâtre de la Porte-Saint-Martin, Jean Toussaint Merle, to a dramatic transfiguration of Polidori's story, *Le Vampire*.[2] The end-result bore only a slight resemblance to the original, but helped nevertheless in its popularization. The villain's name was further transfigured in that version as Rutwen, presumably for much the same reasons that the Ladvocat version had altered it, establishing a distinction while preserving an obvious link.[3]

The Porte-Saint-Martin play, which premiered on June 13, 1820, was a sensational success, and prompted several exercises in imitation, including a similarly-titled melodrama by Pierre de la Fosse, an opera by Joseph Ramoux with music by Heinrich Marschner, and a whole series of parodies, the most notable of which was a "vaudeville" co-written by Eugène Scribe.[4] It helped to

---

[2] Included in *Lord Ruthen the Vampyre*, q.v.

[3] French readers had no way of knowing that the Anglo-Scottish name Ruthven is actually pronounced "Riven," but Bérard and Nodier could both translate English, so they must have known the meanings of the English words "ruth," "rut," and "wen."

[4] Included in *Lord Ruthen the Vampyre*, q.v.

found a tradition of fantastic melodrama at the Porte-Saint-Martin, which proved so stubbornly enduring that when one of Merle's successors ran into trouble 30 years later, he commissioned Alexandre Dumas—who had been present at the first version's première and claimed in his autobiography to have seen Nodier being thrown out at the intermission for heckling—to write a new version of it. Dumas' *Le Vampire*—which retains "Lord Ruthwen" but not much else from its predecessors—premièred in 1851, and helped to spark a further wave of interest in literary vampires in France.[5]

Nodier and Merle's play was rapidly re-exported to England, back-translated in J. R. Planché's *The Vampire; or, The Bride of the Isles* (1820). Perhaps more sensitive to the origins of the villain's name, or perhaps because his company had a stock of kilts to hand, Planché relocated the action to Scotland; he also made the play into a musical, more in the spirit of Scribe's vaudeville than the original. It is probably relevant to note in this context that Bérard's text, which contains a number of songs, does bear some resemblance to a script for a musical; given Bérard's occupation and certain peculiar mannerisms, it is not impossible that it was initially conceived with some such destiny in mind and that its formulation as a novel for Ladvocat was an improvisatory revision. At any rate, Planché also made a contribution to the transformation of the substance of Polidori's story into the stuff of modern legend.

Within this hectic context, the published version of Bérard's sequel seems a frail and muddled effort. Seen from a purely literary viewpoint, it undoubtedly deserves

---

[5] Included in *The Return of Lord Ruthen*, q.v.

the oblivion into which it rapidly slipped. This is not surprising, as it must have been compiled in a tearing hurry; the bulk of the text consists of unrelated stories that Bérard must have composed previously, which were shoveled into the text to bulk it out, under the pretext of employing the "Galland method" of nesting stories within a frame, initially popularized by the French version of *Les Mille et une nuits* (1704-16) and much-imitated. The fact that two of the interpolated stories are unfinished—one of them falling well short of its foreshadowed denouement—presumably results from the fact that Bérard had previously abandoned them in that condition rather than from any innovative literary daring. The introductory narrative and the sections that Bérard wrote to connect up his fragments into an apparent whole are merely a reprise of the fundamental narrative device of Polidori's story, whose further potential (which other subsequent writers proved to be abundant) went largely unexploited—especially in the extremely hurried conclusion, which is little more than a synopsis; it must surely have been composed in confrontation with an exceedingly tight deadline. It is not surprising that the optimistic promise of a sequel appended to the narrative went unfulfilled.

There is also no doubt, however, that one should not, and surely cannot now, look at *Lord Ruthwen* purely from a literary viewpoint; it is more accurately and more interestingly seen as a minor, but crucial, element of a rapidly-grow edifice of revisionist mythology. Despite its literary faults—and, to some extent, because of them—*Lord Ruthwen* is a fascinating text, and it publication in English fills an important gap in the history of vampire fiction, which has lately become interesting to a considerable number of readers and scholars. Its *gauche-*

rie provides remarkably clear evidence of the perceived difficulties facing writers of vampire fiction in the early 19th century, which are spelled out explicitly in Nodier's preliminary observations. Thanks to Polidori, Nodier and Bérard—and also, albeit indirectly, to Lord Byron—later writers had a pattern of established clichés to guide them in their efforts (or, of course, conscientiously to avoid) and to give them and their publishers confidence in the acceptability of such narratives. The underlying fascination of the notion was never in doubt, thanks to the abundant borrowing of materials from Dom Augustine Calmet's pioneering dissertation on the subject, published in 1746.

In connection with the anticipated difficulties spelled out by Nodier, the attempts made within Bérard's narrative to discuss the symbolism of the vampire, in the hope of explaining that fascination, as well as the tentative attempts to extend that symbolism to female vampires, are of particular interest; if nothing else, they help to cast some light on the logic of the extraordinary literary elaboration of the motif that succeeded the spinoff of Polidori's original venture.

Lord Ruthven, as echoed in his shadowy analogues, Lord Ruthwen and Lord Rutwen, was not the first literary character to transcend his text of origin and become malleable clay for other hands—he was following in the footsteps of Faust, among others—but he was the most prominent of his own era. He it was, along with his further mimics, who cemented the image of the male vampire as a Byronic caricature, who remained somehow ominous despite the fact that, from the very outset, he was manifestly absurd. *Lord Ruthwen* wrestles with that absurdity as well as recognizing it, and in so doing helps to demonstrate why *The Vampyre* and its spinoff texts

formulated one of the most widely-familiar literary arc-
hetypes of its era—and why that archetype's subsequent
offspring, in far outdoing its literary achievement, succeeded in contributing further to its notoriety.

Lord Ruthven/Ruthwen/Rutwen's most obvious illegitimate children include the penny-dreadful villain
Varney the Vampyre (1845-47), Marie Nizet's *Le Capi-
taine Vampire* (1879),[6] and, of course, Bram Stoker's
Dracula (1897) as well as numerous lesser individuals.

It was, however, Bérard's text, rather than Polidori's, that foreshadowed, albeit very timidly, the other
major thread of subsequent vampire fiction: the "distaff
side" of the family, featuring seductive female revenants,
as popularized in Étienne Lamothe-Langon's *La Vampire, ou la Vierge de Hongrie* (1825), Théophile Gauti-
er's "La Morte amoureuse" (1836; tr. as "Clarimonde"),
Victor-Alexis Ponson du Terrail's *La Baronne trépassée*
(1852)[7], and Paul Féval's *La Vampire* (1856)[8].

Bérard's female revenants are, admittedly, not particularly seductive, and not particularly dangerous (the
two factors are not unconnected), and might therefore be
considered to flatter only to deceive, but his mock-
reluctant admission of the possibility of female vampires
is perhaps most interesting in its introduction of a notion
that did not catch on. Bettina, returned from her grave, is
not so much a vampire as an "anti-vampire:" the remedy

---

[6] Translated by Brian Stableford and published by Black Coat
Press as *Captain Vampire*; ISBN 9781934543016.

[7] Translated by Brian Stableford and published by Black Coat
Press as *The Vampire and the Devil's Son*; ISBN
9781932983555.

[8] Translated by Brian Stableford and published by Black Coat
Press as *The Vampire Countess*; ISBN 9780974071152.

that eventually facilitates Ruthwen's belated destruction. It is easy to understand why that essentially weak-kneed idea could not thrive in a melodramatic context, but it is an interesting experiment nevertheless, and adds a useful touch of originality to a text that is otherwise, and understandably, rather conservative.

For all its faults, *Lord Ruthwen* remains a significant stepping-stone in the evolution of the modern image of the vampire, and warrants translation and examination of that score.

This translation was made primarily from the version of the Ladvocat text put on line at the Bibliothèque Nationale's website *gallica*, but two pages of that version are missing (the last page of the introduction and the first page of the text proper), so I filled those in from the version placed on line by Oxford University Library and available at *archive.org*.

The text provided some unusual difficulties, firstly because the difficulty of opening the BN copy flat meant that some of the printed characters on the edge of the text were obscured, and had to be deduced from context, secondly because of the inevitable difficulty of translating the rhymed "songs" with which Bérard peppers his narrative, and thirdly, because of the way in which the narrative continually switches back and forth between the present and past historic tenses. Such tense-switches are by no means unusual in French narrative, where the present tense is often used to heighten dramatic passages in texts that are otherwise couched in the past historic, but Bérard's are uncommonly frequent and seemingly arbitrary (hence my suggestion above that the text might have been based on a sketch for a play; the fact that the interpolated stories share the same peculiarity might reflect a similar origin). Whatever the reason, though, the text sometimes switches several times within a single paragraph, and frequently changes within the span of a single sentence. Although I have conserved the eccentric spirit of the original by retaining almost all of these switches, I have eliminated a few that seemed to me to be errors of carelessness or forgetfulness rather than deliberate moves.

Although I have tried to be as accurate as is feasible in translating the words of Bérard's text into fluent English, I have altered its layout quite considerably, breaking up his longer paragraphs (some of which contain as many as 30 items of dialogue in the original) and introducing extra text-breaks and headings that will hopefully assist the reader to cope with its awkward structure.

Brian Stableford

Preliminary Observations

It is perhaps essential, when one publishes a novel of this sort, to reply in advance to the inevitable objection of criticism by means of a frank confession. The story you are about to read belongs to the Romantic genre that is so obstinately, and perhaps justly, decried. The only justification that can be made in favor of the choice is that no novel was known to the ancients that could be considered as a classical model, and that Aristotle does not appear to have taken the trouble to trace the rules of this kind of composition.[9]

Even the name *novel*, suggestive of modern language, modern literature and a modern era of the imagination and sentiment, excludes the obligation of the servile imitation of antiquity that is the universal and abso-

---

[9] Although more than one contemporary compiler of books of advice to writers has attempted to draw upon the structural analyses contained in Aristotle's *Poetics*, those analyses focus specifically on Greek drama. The only other narrative genre to which Aristotle paid any attention was epic poetry, which has no particular structure, being long on story and short on plot. As Nodier observes, there was no long prose fiction available to him, but it might be worth noting that there was a structural-ly-interesting genre of short fiction, comprising fables and apologues, which he ignored completely, perhaps because his great rival Plato, with whom Aristotle made it a point of principle to disagree, had made constructive use of apologues in *The Symposium* and *The Republic*—a stratagem that Aristotle was unwilling or unable to adopt.

21

lute condition of beauty in all the arts.[10] We are, in fact, too far away from the naïve ideas of early eras to take pleasure in the pastoral amours of Longus's hero, as recounted in the delightful story of Daphnis and Chloe, who has lost his plausibility along with his models. Thanks to the improvement of our mores, the majority of ordinary readers of novels reject the cynical depictions of the most elegant imitators of Lucian or Petronius. If one of these genres has long ceased to be classical, because it has ceased to be true, and if the other has never been classical for honest folk because it has never been moral, it is necessary to seek another type for the modern novel in the present character of our civilization, and another source of aspiration in our most commonplace sentiments, our most pronounced passions and our most poetic superstitions.

Far be it from me to consider as a theme very favorable to the imagination and good taste those superstitions which, regretfully admitted by peoples, offer nothing to the intellect but scenes of terror. Such subjects doubtless ought only to be approached with timid sobrie-

---

[10] This statement reads more convincingly in English than French, because the English word "novel" really is suggestive of modernity, whereas the French *roman*—which can equally well be translated "romance"—is not. The term *roman* was, however, an adaptation of the term invented to describe Medieval romances, which were still see in early-19th century France as example of essentially "popular" fiction rather than "classical" literary models. Modern apologues, such as Voltaire's *contes philosophiques*, were also considered to be mimicking the popular form of the *conte* [folktale] rather than Platonic models, although attitudes might have been different had Aristotle included apologues in his analysis of literary practice.

ty. However, the frightful fable of vampirism could not avoid being consecrated in all the nations that are familiar with it in a few romantic tales. It is found in several episodes of the Arabian Nights. It has furnished lyrical elegies, the solemn horror of which is further augmented by the monotonous gravity of a bizarre rhythm, among the Slavs of the Adriatic islands. Finally, it has recently transfixed the attention of Europe in favor of a name that recommends all the writings to which it is attached: that of Lord Byron. Today, for the first time, it has furnished a developed composition to our literary medium.

That is perhaps enough, and the delicate circumspection that distinguishes the French mind necessarily advises our writers that they should be miserly with the future of this bold resource, useful at most in the arousal of a blasé sensitivity or to irritate a reluctant curiosity to sensation. I thought, nevertheless, when I was consulted on this subject that two motives, which excuse everything in France, will excuse the author's attempt. One is the merit of pertinence, the other that of a difficulty overcome. I have no doubt that the public will agree with me on another kind of merit this novel possesses, which is rarer and more estimable. I think I also recognize in it a great richness of imagination, a piquant variety of episodes, and a sustained elegance of style, and I regard my publisher's invitation to associate myself with its publication as a favor.

C.N.

Part One
The Story of Bettina and Léonti

I

Venice, the bold situation of which seems beyond human imagination, rises up as if by magic in the middle of the sea. Its celebrity dates from centuries already remote, and, redoubtable to all peoples, its far-traveling flag has long advertised to strange lands its respected naval power, the number of its seamen and the imposing memory of a glory that is no more.

Simultaneously menaced and protected by the waves of the Adriatic, which surrounds it on all sides, Venice presents to the astonished eye a frightful spectacle of severity. Not far from its lagoons, however, by virtue of a contrast that enchants the heart and the eye, hospitable woods embellish an ever-lovely nature linking the Lido to a few striking and delightfully cool areas of verdure.

It is on this fortunate isle that young Bettina lives. It is there, impatient with hope and love, that she awaits the lover for whose absence she has wept, and with whom she would like to be united forever.

It is midnight. The beautiful Italian sky, pure and starry, still brightens the environs of Venice. The moon outlines in the distance the majestic architecture of the Doge's palace, a precious monument of the Middle Ages, and its melancholy light strikes falls upon the gondoliers' huts. At the Lido, the dwelling of their chief is distinguished by its extent, and shines with a new

25

gleam. Garlands of flowers suspended from the trees, set tables, elegantly-decorated boats moored on the shore, and various preparations all around, advertise an impending fête.

All is calm; everyone is asleep. Only a light wind troubles the silence of the nearby wood. The hour is conducive to sweet dreams and amorous mysteries.

A window opens. Bettina appears. Alone in the middle of the night, no fabric veils her charms. The linen that protects them without hiding them adds to her beauty. Her black hair, descending over her shoulders, augments the pallor of her face, giving all her features a more touching expression. Her abandoned bed calls to her in vain.

What grief has wrenched her from slumber? What sentiment is it that agitates her? Is it regret for a possession lost without hope of recovery, or the intoxication that precedes a long-desired happiness? A vague anxiety is painted in her eyes. Attentive, scarcely breathing, she gazes at the sea, which unfurls an unknown extent before her sight. Every slight sound fading away in the atmosphere—the toll of a solitary church-bell, the cry of a bird in the woods, the swell that rises and the wave that breaks—presents to her an image that charms her, a hope that excites her.

Suddenly, her bosom swells, her face colors and her voice resounds. With her eyes and gesture, she indicates a distant object that seems to be coming closer. She thinks she is seeing a floating boat. She thinks so, and already she is calling out to an adored lover. Vain illusion! It is an isolated rock, whose shadow, reproduced in the water, seems at first to be moving, but soon remains still.

Bettina recognizes her error, and her oppressed heart lets slip a sigh.

O surprise, though! A gentle harmony is heard. Who comes at this hour to repeat a song of love? Why hide? Is it a foreign lover? Is it Léonti? The wood hides him from Bettina's gaze. What a mystery! She listens. Alas, the voice is unfamiliar.

> Ah, what a pleasant delight,
> On a long voyage home one feels,
> As one's native shore shines bright;
> The distant horizon reveals,
> Parading before hopeful sight
> The village church, whose bell peals.
> For the impatient returnee
> All is pleasure, all is glee.
> Everything charms his avid soul
> Every element enchants the whole
> Every step sets his heart ablaze
> And reminds him of youth's days:
> Woodland flowers, the green field,
> The tree, the hill, the sacred stone
> Where his first homage was sealed
> And his first farewell was a moan.
> Bettina!

"O Heaven!" Bettina cries. "Léonti!"

Scarcely has this cry escaped her than everything— the song, the harmony—ceases; and like a dream, a vague sensory delirium whose transient illusion is destroyed by an awakening, everything has disappeared.

Bettina lends an ear again. Profound silence. Only an echo replies to her voice, and Léonti's name expires in the distance on the shore. It is not him, then. But who is this mysterious lover who has fled at the name of a preferred rival? Will he be generous enough not to make her repent of being imprudently betrayed by a single word, the indiscreet confession of a heart too full of the one it loves?

To deliver oneself to sentiments that it is necessary both to hide and feel; to develop a need for apprehension; to make a habit of constraint; to find an accustomed charm in painful dreams and a continual torment in one's most cherished affections; to be saddened by a gaze, made anxious by a smile; to betray oneself with a word, console oneself with a tear, and, on the point of obtaining a promised happiness, to experience every day, at every hour, at every moment, a thousand dreads troubling hope—such is the fate of women in a life that, agitated by long periods of grief and successes of short duration, passes rapidly, leaving no time for direction, and who, beginning with errors, escape ennui by means of memories, flee through the forgetfulness of others, and lose themselves in regret.

II

Bettina loved Léonti. Born on the same shore, they had spent their early years together. Their love was deceived by time and obstacles. A quarrel over unimportant interests, a rivalry of state, divided their families, once united by an amity that appeared to be proof against all the stormy events of life.

Soon, Léonti, refused by his beloved's father and deprived, while still young, of an adored mother, left the abode of his forefathers and sought a refuge from unhappiness in a military career. He hoped that glory might one day wipe away the tears of love, and that Torelli would accord to a defender of Venice that which an unjust hatred had made him refuse to a simple gondolier.

To vanquish that resistance, he also had powerful support from Bettina's mother. The good Verina cherished her daughter, and protected the two lovers, so it was to that tender mother that the young Venetian woman entrusted the care of her happiness—and her happiness was entirely dependent on becoming the wife of the man who, in opening her heart to love, had given birth to her first disquiet and decided the destiny of her life.

Léonti had already fought for the fatherland, and his regiment, having been recalled, had arrived a few days ago. He had announced his return to Venice and promised to appear at the gondoliers' fête. He knew that everything was prepared for the celebration, and that in the midst of various games, tumultuous scenes of gaiety and Venetian dances, he ought to be able to offer himself to his beloved's eyes and obtain a secret meeting with her.

29

That was the matter that absorbed all Bettina's thoughts.

Reason sleeps when love awakes. Torelli's daughter has told her secret to the infidel winds; she has confided her distress to the calm of the night; and her impatient vows have anticipated the dawn.

Finally, day breaks. The atmosphere is split by cries of joy. Its oar rapidly plied, a gondola prepared by skillful hands flies away from the shore. The repetitive barcarole mingles with the lively music of the guitar, whose docile strings leap beneath the hand that presses them, and the distant echo of the shore, like an imitative instrument, asserts yet again that the inspirational soil of Italy is the fatherland of melodious song.

Everywhere, the scene is animated. Everyone surrenders to joy. Bettina alone is pensive. Insensible to the homages that her elegant figure and adornment attract, to the cries of admiration that burst forth around her, she sees and hears nothing. She does not suspect that her distracted attitude embellishes her, that her melancholy distributes a new charm over her entire person; when she dances, her lightness and magical grace are applauded, but she does not notice. Meanwhile, her troubled eyes are moistened involuntarily; a tear falls, and betrays the secret of her sadness. One sole idea possesses her. The fête is wearing on, and Léonti has not arrived.

Suddenly, a stranger appears. His costume and aristocratic mannerisms reveal an elevated rank, but his distorted features and wild gaze give the lie to the tranquility that he is striving to manifest, and his furrowed brow gives evidence to all eyes that his life has been tormented by frightful chagrin. He is greeted with respectful urgency; he is asked what he wants.

He replies in these terms: "Fleeing the unwelcome tumult of cities, I have come to the shore where you dwell. I was wandering in your woods—a sweet shelter, a cool refuge—when joyful sounds suddenly struck my ears. Scenes of happiness exert an attraction upon me that I cannot resist. That is why I headed in this direction. Continue your games; I have no wish to disturb them."

Reassured by what he has said, the dancers begin again.

The stranger has noticed Bettina immediately. At the sight of her beauty, which has the freshness of a new flower, his face conserves its livid pallor but an interior fire had reddened his lips, and his smile is frightful. He approaches her, questions her interestedly, divines the cause of the anxiety of a heat unskillful in hiding its rapid impressions. He sympathizes with her, consoles her, offers her his help, and, effortlessly captures her confidence, which is too prompt to surrender to hasty concern and kind attention.

Heaven's most beautiful gift is innocence, but it is defenseless against the poisonous charm of seduction, and, like a flower of the fields beaten by the autumn wind, is permanently wilted in an instant.

Meanwhile, the feast continues. While the dancers are resting, a Tyrolean woman has come into their midst. She gives an account of her errant life, her success in foreign lands, and says that her magical art allows her to predict the future. Immediately, groups form around her.

People pretend to listen to these popular oracles indifferently, but such is the attraction of everything that is outside the common run and touches on the marvelous that, on the word of a vagabond fortune-teller, chatelaines and shepherdesses are equally afflicted by the

31

chagrin with which an impure mouth threatens them, and rejoice in an uncertain happiness announced with confidence. In this way, credulity has often been seen to bring fear into a palace, and hope into a cottage.

The Tyrolean woman's pronouncements awaken amusement and interest, but no one dares to consult her at first. Her presence inspires a thousand secret projects in hopeless lovers and faithless spouses, and more than one young heart, fearful of losing that which it loves, would like to find in the confidence of a propitious fortune the imminent end of the anguish that torments it.

Skillful in reading the thoughts behind the gazes that strive to interrogate her, Elmoda is aware of the hope and read she inspires. She waves her mysterious wand in the air, composes her gestures, her expression and her voice, and launches into a prophetic improvisation:

"O you who surround me, listen to my songs.

"I speak to you of the prodigies of an art whose origin is lost in the traditions of ancient times. The stars consulted in the fields of Chaldea, the mysteries honored on the Egyptian shore and the famous oracles of Greece have revealed their redoubtable secrets to us.

"Messengers sent to this earth of exile, a supernatural power has appointed us the arbiters of human destiny.

"Peoples, address your prayers to us! Kings of the earth, bow down before our savant inspiration.

"Our predictions are infallible. They say to the prideful who triumph, hope for nothing more from fortune; to the weak, hope once more; to the virtuous, you shall remain pure and respected forever, if you remain forever neglected.

"We predict a glorious death to courage, inconstant slavery to beauty, abandonment to unhappiness, success to intrigue, disgrace to fidelity.

"All of you, who wish to know your fate, appear before me! My gaze will penetrate the utmost depths of your hearts."

Elmoda's song has ended. The gondolier remains motionless, the young lover has shivered, and the voice of roving oracles, which appeals for confidence in vain, has already spread fear around. But the attention of the Tyrolean sibyl has fixed itself upon the distinguished appearance of the stranger. She advances toward him.

"My lord," she says, "would you like to know your future? I will even tell you everything that has happened to you before today."

"No," the stranger replies, in a severe tone. Then, turning to Bettina, he adds: "Open that beautiful hand and hold it out, young woman. Why are you trembling?"

"You are greatly troubled, dear child. You're waiting for someone. It's a lover."

"A husband," said Torelli.

"What! Father..."

"He sang last night beneath your window. I heard him. He was born in the next village, but he spent his youth among us."

"What is his name?"

"Tomaso. I have promised him your hand, and I'm astonished that he has not come to the feast."

"He will come," the Tyrolean woman says to Bettina.

"Who?"

"The man you love."

Bettina replies with a sigh.

"Wait—your fate interests me. I want to penetrate the entire mystery."

Elmoda takes her magical pictures from her bosom then, on which various characters are traced; she shuffles them, consults them, demands complete silence, and continues her examination. Vivid emotion is painted in all her features. Her eyes have become wild, her hands tremble, her mouth quivers.

"Great God! I see…"

"What do you see?" several voices repeat.

"A misfortune; a frightful crime."

"Speak!"

"This young woman…"

"Bettina?"

"Yes—soon, Bettina is going to die!"

At these words, a cry emerges from the woods. A young soldier clears a path through the crowd, launches himself forward and addresses the Tyrolean woman: "Wretch! What do you dare to say…?"

It is Léonti.

An extreme pallor covers Bettina's face. Her strength abandons her.

"Yes," Elmoda continues, "her days are numbered. Her blood will be drained, drop by drop. Tremble for her, tremble, O you who surround me! Flee, all of you."

"Let us flee!"

"Know that a vampire…"

"O Heaven!" says Léonti. "A vampire! Is it possible? Speak, where is he, then?"

"He is on this shore, among you, in this very place and he is…"

"Stop, imprudent woman," says the stranger, fixing her with a terrible gaze. "Cease these impostures. It's money you want—here it is. Earn your living without

34

predicting the death of others. Go away, or fear my wrath."

"O Bettina!" cries Léonti, beside himself, "my beloved Bettina, wake up. It's me—me, your lover—who is begging you, hugging you, covering you with tears. It's in vain that your life has been threatened. Who would dare, when I live to adore you and to defend you? Come, have no fear; believe in my love and my rage. Before anyone could reach you, my arm would be prompt to avenge you, and this sword, more rapid than an arrow that cleaves the air, would have plunged into the heart of the guilty party a thousand times."

Everyone has fled. Even the Tyrolean woman has run away. Torelli and Verina are chilled by fear. Bettina has recovered consciousness. Her astonishment is extreme. Her smile, on which unhappiness imprints a divine sweetness; her virginal brow, tinted by modesty; her embarrassment and the agitation it causes—everything within her testifies that she has no thought other than for the lover she adores, and the happiness of being close to him, in his arms. The rest seems to have been effaced from her memory. An alarmed mother is supporting her. Léonti reassures her, lavishing the most tender names upon her. Her hand trembles in his. Her father sees that, understands it, and his gaze has nothing severe in it.

"Come," says the stranger, then, "let's get away from this unwelcome crowd. Forget a vain terror. Are you unfamiliar with the audacity of these women, who, avid for a shameful wage, will stop at nothing to obtain it? Not daring to judge the present, which is easier to interrogate, they charge a future impenetrable to all eyes with the disorders of their delirious imagination. By that means they interest timid minds in their deceptive predictions. How credulous humans are! How passion leads them astray! What weakness there is in those creatures, so proud in prosperity and so abject, so pitiful, at the slightest dread of an anticipated reverse! Let us be careful of young Bettina's sensibility, however. Her heart is only too likely to receive sad impressions. Come, Torelli, let's go to your house. I know everything that interests you, and I want to offer you the advice of a friend."

And both of them, engaged in animated conversation, have soon traversed the distance that they have to travel.

At that moment, Léonti cannot help feeling a surge of jealousy and suspicion. The stranger worries him. Bettina hastens to dispel his suspicions. "He will be our protector," she says. "He promised me that. As you see, he's speaking to my father, whose agreement is today a happy anticipation—and if, by virtue of his concern, his pleas and the respect he inspires, he succeeds in uniting me with all that I love, I shall owe him more than life. O Léonti, dear object of all my desires! O Mother…!"

She can no longer speak. She is weeping. They are tears of sweet joy.

Poor Bettina! Her throbbing heart surrenders to the most delightful hope. Perhaps…

III

Bettina and Léonti arrive at Torelli's house. They take their places around a table set for the evening meal—and there, by means of his persuasive tongue, the stranger flatters the generosity of his host, encourages the two lovers, calms a mother's anxieties, and charms all his listeners.

But all Léonti's thoughts, to begin with, are devoted to the danger to be run by his dear Bettina, calmer now; he recalls the tumult that brought the feast to an end. Elmoda's last words are incessantly present in his mind, and a deadly presentiment pursues him, obsessing him in spite of himself. He tries to guess who the vampire that she wanted to identify might be.

The word vampire, in itself, causes a secret terror within him that he cannot get over. He is in doubt, unable to comprehend that men exist capable of all the horrors that are attributed to those monsters, invisible destroyers of a sex, the admirable ornament of life, whose weakness is already subjected to so many perils.

He questions the stranger, who smiles, and hastens to reply to him in a friendly manner.

"History," the stranger says, "in unfurling before our eyes the overthrow of empires and the revolutions of peoples, progresses through successive centuries surrounded by great truths and various fictions. The former are lessons that are forgotten, the latter fabulous depictions that delight, and are reproduced in different forms. There are errors dear to popular credulity, and which even contribute to the recreations of the elevated social classes. On harsh winter evenings, when snow falls in billows, rain in torrents, or storm-winds shake the forest trees, the weary woodcutter takes his rest by the unsteady light of a flickering fire; he scolds his young family, huddled around him by fear, and even he, listing avidly to a gripping tale, believes that he sees phantoms wandering in ruins, while merry lies alleviate the evening tedium of the château.

"For a long time it was believed that vampirism was a symbol of the perversity of men and the fatality associated with virtuous beings. All too often, the word offers images of ingratitude and corruption, overwhelming with their unexpected success the innocence that succumbs and the fidelity that moans in oblivion. It is said that men betrayed, unhappy in life, dying with vengeance in their hearts, return after their death to advertise their passage everywhere with bloody scenes. It is more consoling, however, to think that Heaven, limiting the number of these pitiless beings, has wanted to show them to the world in order to engrave more forcefully upon the hearts of other men a horror of crime and the sentiment of an eternal life, and, as divine bounty is reluctant to produce such monsters twice over, has permitted the same souls, recovering mortal coil, to reappear to desolate the earth.

"Strangers to remorse and pity, vampires choose for victims those creatures who are most charming in their delightful form, most interesting in their weakness, and most enchanting in their beauty. Like a woodland bird which, subjected to a spell that attracts it, and whose danger it cannot avoid, hops regretfully from branch to branch, unable to take flight as usual, advances involuntarily, halts, utters a dolorous cry, and finally falls in front of the reptile that swallows it, the woman soon falls prey to the vampire that follows her step by step."

"O Heaven!" said Léonti. "Can the Earth not be liberated from these monsters?"

"There are no certain signs by which they may be recognized, and, by virtue of a bizarrerie whose counterpart in not unexampled in society, they hide their perfidy beneath the most attractive exterior."

"So they do exist?"

"I am obliged to believe so," the stranger continued, "as you may judge by an event to which I was witness. I love traveling, and in order to vary my pleasures, I never return to countries that I have visited. Nothing gives greater extent to human conceptions than the renewed depiction of the character, mores and customs of peoples. Intellect grows by means of the comparison of so many various objects, and the fire of genius reignites to pain in broad stokes the romantic beauty spots of Provence, the cheerful landscapes of Italy, the arid soil of deserts and the icy climes of Moscow.

"I had been travelling in the vast empire of the Czars, and when, on my return, I passed through the ancient city of Koenigsberg, bathed by the green-tinted waters of the Spregel, the horizon revealed to my sight clouds that were confused with the immensity of the Baltic. That imposing sea, rival of the Adriatic, ever replete with sailors and bold navigators, opens its industrious ports to the riches of two worlds.

"After devoting a few days to examining all the precious produce acquired by the insatiable cupidity of humans, I continued on my way, and, skirting the shady banks of the Vistula, laid my observant eyes upon the fertile countryside of Poland. That beautiful province, so jealous of its liberty, is populated by involuntary agriculturalists who are born and die in servitude. Beside a hearth suspended on heaped stones, a crude edifice constructed by unskilled hands, the Pole, enveloped in a thick fur, seems more numbed by sloth than by the harsh cold of winter.

"Sparse châteaux, the only habitations open to hospitality, announce that opulence is the prerogative of powerful families, and oppression the law that an invincible necessity imposes on all the rest. In the season when frost covers the earth, a profound solitude reigns throughout the fields of Poland. Nature there seems to be a vast desert in which one only finds trees whitened by snow, a few vestiges of half-erased footprints, and he breath of the north wind, a mobile compass often replaced by a rising breeze. The traveler, wandering without a guide, interrogates these feeble indications of a road for whose races, lost beneath the ice, he searches in vain.

"It is then that the troublesome aspect of inhabited countries inspires the soul with fearful meditations. That bleakness extends all the way to the gates of Warsaw. There, everything changes: an immense city, floods of people spreading out in every direction, varied scenes and magnificent palaces astonish the gaze everywhere. Only the gaudy adornment of horses obedient to the reins that guide them advertises from afar the raid passage of sleighs disappearing over the snow that yields to their imperceptible effort, and the elegant Polish women, protected by a costume around which shines ermine whiter than the moving ground that they tread with their elegant feet, display their slender forms and charming faces to the enchanted eye…

"Forgive me if I paint with enthusiasm places in which my heart filled up with memories whose sweetness nothing can disturb, allowing me to forget the story that I was about to tell you.

"Obliged to leave Poland, I was already twenty miles from Warsaw; my carriage, having gone astray on the snow-covered roads, suddenly came to a halt. It was dark; the horses could go no further. The postillion pointed out a château and urged me to go seek shelter there. I decided to do so.

"A door stood ajar; I went in. No domestic servant appeared. I called out; there was no response. The château was inhabited, though; bright light illuminated an apartment perceptible in the distance through the trees in the grounds. I walked in that direction, not without some reluctance. The silence that surrounded me even inspired a little fear.

"Finally, I arrived, and found, next to an elegantly-laid table, a young woman of dazzling beauty, inanimate in an armchair. Head bowed, as if surprised by sleep, she had surrendered to an involuntary drowsiness. At first, everything confirmed that initial impression: four children were with her; one was covering her with caresses and weeping, two others were calling to her, and a girl scarcely out of childhood was trying to make them be quiet. She ran toward me as soon as she noticed me, and said to me with touching ingenuousness: 'Mama needs rest, Monsieur; she has wept so much today; don't wake her up—see, she's asleep.'

"Surprised by the scene before my eyes, I interrogated the girl. She replied: 'We were at supper; a friend of Mama's was with us. He spoke, Mama wept. He drew nearer to her—and, I don't know why, that nasty man frightened me! At last, he went away. Mama went pale, and wrote briefly on this piece of paper. Suddenly, she cried *Elisca!*—that's my name—and I ran to her knee. She looked at me, and her expression scared me—and then…that's when she went to sleep.'

41

"A sinister suspicion took hold of me then. I took the piece of paper from Elisca's hands. I read it. It contained a few lines traced with difficulty. I remember them. This is what they said: *The monster! I have given him hospitality. I am doomed. He has betrayed me. I loved him, and he has murdered me. I no longer have any but a vestige of life...my strength is exhausted. My blood has been drained. O my poor children! What will become of you? O Heaven, have pity! Elisca!*

"I examined the unfortunate mother. I tried to bring her round. Vain assistance! She was no longer alive. She had been the victim of a vampire."

"A vampire?" said Torelli.

"I saw him, in person."

"In person," added Léonti, quivering with anger.

"He came back, picked up the girl, who threw herself upon him to strike him with her feeble hands—and soon that pretty Elisca, the image of a nascent flower withered on its stem by a scorching wind, had ceased to live. I hastened to run away from that frightful spectacle."

"What!" cried Léonti. "You didn't bury a dagger in the villain's heart?"

"Impossible."

"It was at least necessary to hand him over to the law."

"I had a reason that I cannot tell you for treating him with less rigor," the stranger replied, smiling. "But it's getting late. Let's withdraw, young man. Goodnight, worthy Torelli. Until we meet again, charming Bettina."

IV

To what confused sentiments has all that he had seen and heard given birth in Léonti's soul! An involuntary sadness, the indication of an imminent unhappiness, throws him into a profound distress. He follows the stranger; he is close behind him—and the path they follow escapes his attention.

This time, as he draws away from Bettina, he experiences an inexplicable anxiety. His heart beats faster, especially at the moment when the gondola that is to take them to Venice quits the cherished shore of the Lido. An inexpressible anguish grips him.

The immense sea that offers itself to his sight in every direction; the calm of the night; perhaps even one of those fatal presentiments, the secret warnings of Heaven that import a sharp disturbance into the soul's depths, against which the human mind tries in vain to rebel—everything enhances and redoubles his misery. But then, by virtue of a contrast that is only too frequent in the foreground of life, a joyous prelude becomes audible beside him.

The boat is flying, scarcely skimming the water's surface, and the gondolier has already sung the chorus of a favorite barcarole of the young women of the Lido. Soon he sings.

"The standard of Venice calls you to distant shores. Depart, O gondolier! But forget not the fatherland where you were born for glory where you were loved for your good fortune. If fate betrays your courage, to console yourself, remember the beauty that mourns your absence; and, if you return victorious in battle, fear not to entrust your impatience to the fragile hull in which you must brave the waves of an angry sea. Hasten; you are awaited. A loving kiss will be your recompense. Then, O gondolier, lay your armor down on the shore, take up your guitar, and sing the song of happiness again."[11]

At these lines, which seem to describe perils and hopes that he has known himself, Léonti emerges from his profound reverie. He listens. The gondolier repeats his chorus, strikes the waves with his oar, and continues a song that Venetian suffrage has rendered popular.

"Young lover! Hymen has crowned your vows. The virginal face of your beloved is covered at the sight of you by the charm of a transient modesty. Hear its song of love. Elegant and pure, its voice mingles your name, which causes it to shiver, with the religious oath. The flowing wave is less gentle in its course, morning bird-song no more touching, and already it is done; Rosella is yours. Discreet in love, she loves you without saying so; fortunate spouse, she might yet love you more and tell you always. O gondolier, sing your happiness!"

That said, ceding of its own accord to repeated efforts, the gondola reaches the shore.

On setting foot on Venetian soil, Bettina's lover sighs, as his heart has not strength enough to throw off the vague sense of sadness by which he is overwhelmed. The stranger, who has not said a word since their departure from the Lido, and has shown himself equally in-

---

[11] It is not obvious why these lines are not rendered in rhyming verse like most of the other songs featured in the narrative. It may be that this is a literal translation of an actual Venetian ballad, or the lines might be a rough draft of a poem that Bérard had not yet formulated in rhyme.

sensible to Léonti's groans and the gondolier's songs, finally breaks his silence.

"I am going to cause you distress," he said. "A friend sometimes has a painful duty to fulfill; you interest me, and I ought to tell you your fate."

"Speak," Léonti replied, swiftly. "I'm ready for anything."

The stranger went on: "Bettina's fainting fit, and the fear that a miserable adventuress was able to inspire in all minds, initially quieted the unjust resentment that Torelli bears against you, but he soon reverted to his original resolution. It was only by virtue of my advice and my strenuous insistence that he consented to protect his daughter's threatened health and receive you in is home. You have tasted a few moments of a happiness that only had the duration of a dream. Thus it is that, in the midst of the gnawing anxieties of a desperate situation, the slightest glimmer of a less frightful fate momentarily puts to sleep the pain that seems far away, but which will soon return, keener than before, never to leave us again. Such, at any rate, is the misfortune that threatens you. Abandon all hope. Torelli has asked me to tell you to respect the wishes of a father, and not to return again to the places where your mere presence is a source of anxiety."

"What?" said Léonti, sobbing. "Nothing can change his mind! Well, then I shall go away, Yes, I shall go away…but what am I saying? What will become of Bettina? I know her. She will die, and I shall be the cause." In a distraught tone, he cried: "No. no! I will not betray her. I will never abandon her!"

"Well," said the stranger, "in order not to be separated from her, you have only one means remaining."

"What is it? Hurry up and tell me.

"You will have to abduct her."

"Abduct her! Great God! But how, without help?"

"You shall have it."

"Without money?"

"Make use of mine."

"Overgenerous friend!"

"I offer you service in the army of Scotland. You shall leave with a letter to the general in command of it. He is a relative and friend of mine. He will see to your advancement."

"But what about my regiment—my colonel, who holds me in esteem and has taken me under his wing?"

"Your flight will be concealed."

"But my honor!"

"Honor! Frightful reverses have taught me to know men and judge events. One day, you will no longer be led astray by the errors of an ardent youth; then, you will learn, from the cruel experience that age will bring you, that honor, a vain word and a true phantom, is merely the illusion of a disguised pride. Think of your happiness, young man."

"If I can only dream of it by becoming culpable, I renounce it."

"So you're renouncing Bettina?"

"Renouncing Bettina? Impossible!"

"Sign this pledge, then."

"Give it to me; I'll surrender blindly to your advice." *dumbass?!*

"I'll take care of everything."

"You'll cover our flight?"

"A boat will be waiting for you on the shore."

"When?"

"Tomorrow, at daybreak."

"Agreed."

"Count on me."

"Goodbye!" said Léonti, in a stifled voice.

V

The hours of darkness pass by slowly, however. While Léonti is subject to the most intense agitation, Bettina, ignorant of the fate that awaited her on awakening, and worn out by the day's painful scenes, yields to the pressure of a deep sleep.

A pleasant dream stirs her senses delightfully and flatters her imagination, which offers her the seductive imminence of a future full of charm. Her happiness is assured. No more obstacles. Léonti is at her feet, intoxicated by love and joy. He calls her his dearly beloved, his adored wife. Her father leads her to the altar. The priest is about to marry them.

Suddenly, a violent tempest looms. The storm bursts, lightning flashes, thunder rumbles; the portico of the holy temple collapses; everything shatters into smithereens—and Bettina, knocked down, falls unconscious…

She awakes with a start. A stone has stuck her window. She gets up. A voice calls out to her: "I'm waiting for you in the wood."

She opens her heavy eyelids with difficulty, and looks out. There is no one to be seen.

Momentarily, she remains motionless with astonishment. "Is it real? Is it a dream prolonged by illusion? She collects herself. The noise that she heard was no chimera; she recognized Léonti's voice. The words *in the wood* are still echoing in her ears.

Her father is absent; the moment is propitious for going to the indicated spot. She hurriedly puts on her light clothes, but such is the force of the desire to please in women that, even in the midst of a thousand confused ideas, Léonti's young lover devotes some care to the elegant simplicity of her adornment. Her beautiful hair blows free in the morning breeze. A simple ribbon, a pledge of love, retains the charming curls at her neck, whiter than ermine.

She finally leaves, with a tremulous step, for the mysterious rendezvous.

She wandered for some time without finding Léonti. Finally, she perceived him in a sheltered spot close to the shore. He was pale and pensive, his stare, fixed upon the Adriatic, seemingly measuring its extent.

Bettina ran to him and said to him, as she drew near: "What's the matter, dear Léonti? How is it that on seeing me, your dispirited features are painted with anxiety?"

"Say impatience, O Bettina! Today, in a moment, I shall know whether you love me."

"Alas, how can you doubt it?" she replied, with the most passionate abandon and recklessness "Since my mouth has sworn an oath to belong to no one but Léonti, I have never had any other desire, hope or idol but him. In our absence, I have languished in regret, dried up in tears. The anger of a father, so many vows disdained, so many obstacles braved and chagrins suffered—nothing, dear Léonti, has been able, and nothing ever will be able, to stifle in my heart the love that dates back to the cradle of our life."

"Well, arm yourself with courage."

"The time of proofs is past. A kinder fate leaves us nothing to fear, and everything to hope for."

"Disillusion yourself."

"My father saw you here yesterday, without reluctance."

"He pretended to, at least."

"Perhaps he'll consent."

"According to his orders, I must never see you again."

"O Heaven! Who told you that?"

"The stranger."

"The stranger?"

"We must leave."

"Leave! You want to abandon me, Léonti?"

"You shall come with me."

"What are you daring to propose?"

"It's the only course that remains open to us."

"You love Bettina, and you want to dishonor her!"

"I want to save her."

"You claim to be saving me, and you give me the deadly advice to betray my family and my honor? Dear Léonti, I beg you to come back from your aberration. Think of the misfortune that would pursue us everywhere."

"I'm thinking only of Bettina. Everything is prepared for our flight.

"Our flight! No, no—don't expect that."

"Farewell, then."

"Léonti! Don't you recognize this voice any longer, which is so dear to you? You're going? You're running away? You're leaving me alone in this place?"

"You're weeping?"

"Ingrate, that I loved so much!"

"Oh, Bettina, don't try to turn me away from a necessary course. If I stayed, I would be an obstacle to your happiness."

"What are you daring to say?"

"I shall go. I shall flee to distant climes, and there, on the harsh summit of some distant rag, or beneath some uninhabited shelter, the sky alone will be witness to my unbearable dolor. Unfortunate in having loved you, and in admiring you still, more unfortunate in no longer being able to tell you so, ~~devoid of fatherland and refuge~~, awaiting death without seeing around me a single friend on whose tears I can count, my cries will still seek you in the solitude of the desert; ever day my sighs will take flight toward you; my sad voice will name Bettina, and my tears…"

"Stop, Léonti…you're breaking my heart. My blood is already freezing in my veins. Take my hand…can you feel it? It's trembling…it's moist with cold sweat. Léonti! In the name of Heaven, have pity on me!"

"We must part."

"I shan't leave you."

"Come with me."

"I can't."

"Time is pressing; I'm going—goodbye."

"Oh, stay! Listen to a lover who adores you, who is begging you… Look at me, cruel man! I'm dying at your feet."

At that moment, the stranger arrives hurriedly, and informs the two lovers that he has just obtained a favorable promise from Torelli. He urges Léonti to take advantage of this fortunate change of mind.

"He's waiting for you," he adds. "Don't lose a second. We'll follow in your footsteps. Go on ahead—it's necessary. I'll bring your beloved Bettina along directly, to the arms of her father, who is already half-disposed to bend his will and yield to our combined entreaties."

Léonti does not give him time to finish. Animated by the sweetest hope, he leaves—flies—and has soon traversed the distance that separated him from the place where he expects to find the assurance of a happiness so long awaited.

VI

As Léonti comes to the threshold of Torelli's door he slows his pace. He listens. A troop of soldiers has assembled around the gondoliers. Torelli is questioning hem. They are asking for Léonti. He introduces himself.

"We've come to arrest you," he is told.

"Arrest me? Me?"

"You must come with us; those are our orders."

"But what have I done?" Léonti replies, rendered motionless by astonishment.

"You have betrayed Venice by deserting your flag to take service in the army of Scotland."

"What? How can this be? Who has told you that?" says Léonti, paralyzed.

This scene, which has already sown fear, is interrupted by a confused noise that suddenly erupts. A gondolier runs into their midst. Breathless, gripped by terror, he speaks disjointedly. All eyes are upon him.

"Friends," he says, "I've come to tell you...a frightful crime...my boat, launched from the shore...found an obstacle in its path... I looked—O shock! I saw...I'm still shivering in consequence...I saw...a corpse floating in the water...and I recognized the Tyrolean woman who declared at our fête that a vampire was among us!"

"God!" cried Léonti. "What suspicion! What a flash of enlightenment! The Tyrolean woman lifeless, my secret betrayed...yes, it's him! Torelli! Soldiers! Gondoliers! My friends! You shall know everything. Run that way. Search for Bettina and the guilty man. I tremble at the thought that there may no longer be time. Great God! What am I seeing?"

Whimpering, colorless, her hair in disarray, scarcely able to drag herself along, Bettina appears, like a spectre frightful to behold, making one final effort...

"Father! Léonti! Avenge me...the stranger...!"

She is unable to finish. The words expire on her lips. Her last sigh escapes her, and she falls at her mother's feet.

Despair and fury then take possession of every heart. A general cry rises up: "Where is the stranger?"

Léonti can no longer see or hear anything. He runs, ahead of everyone else. Like a furious lion impelled by a devouring hunger, he searches for his prey. Torelli and the gondoliers race after him. His agonized breast can only exhale cries of rage. His voice refuses the movements necessary to speech. He indicates by gestures which way they must go, which man that they must strike down.

They search everywhere. Vengeance inspires every face. A thousand arms are raised to punish the guilty. They hurry, they call out, they run to the shore, they arrive. Vain efforts! The stranger has disappeared.

Thus, happiness is neighbor to extreme misfortune. How often has seen the favorite of an opulent court, heaped with riches and honors, forget that the breath of adversity might cause the blade suspended above his head to fall? All-powerful in the palace of kings, he triumphs, and everyone flatters his vanity at first, everyone smiles at his ambitious vows; in the dizzying whirl of a favor that still seems to be rising and becoming more solid, he is able to dare everything—but at the very moment when he thinks himself secure from any downfall, disgrace arrives, shiny prestige dissipates like a thin vapor; friends, courtesans and protégés all flee with the master's favor; and then, from the steps of the throne, he is thrown into the last asylum of the guilty, astonished by his terrible fall; he is overwhelmed, devoid of hope and unable to understand how he has reached that ultimate degree of misfortune.

Such is Léonti's distress. He sheds no tears, the feeble relief of hearts brushed by a grief that will not last. Great pains are silent. When the entire body is gripped, all the senses suspended by a devouring evil, tears cannot find a way out; they eye is dry, the heart on fire, and a delirious fever absorbs the impulses of a sensibility that lacks the strength to burst forth.

Léonti was on the point of becoming the happiest of men, or at least he thought so, and death has snatched from his arms the woman he adored, the only creature attaching him to the earth. He feels that everything he loves has been betrayed, struck down, annihilated. It is all over for him. mood it's Léover

It is ended; Bettina is no more. Her angelic head is resting on the bosom of a mother who wants to follow a beloved child to her last resting-place. To have all the pleasurable attractions, all the connecting virtues, to be beautiful, charming, in the flower of life…and to die! Vain regrets! A layer of sand will soon cover Léonti's young lover forever. She lived 15 spring times for innocence and love. A single instant sufficed to steal her away from this earth of exile. Thus shine and wither the flowers of the desert.

Léonti has no desire to survive his Bettina. His wild eyes are fixed upon her discolored corpse, which the expression of life and the animated charm of her beauty delighted for a brief interval. After the initial collapse into mute dolor, nature awakes again and his tears flow in abundance. He calls out to a lover who can no longer hear him, his strength exhausting itself in sobs; and, yielding to the violence of his despair, he falls unconscious while pronouncing Bettina's name.

He is carried into Torelli's house; the most generous care is lavished upon him. A few days pass; his condition deteriorates; a continual delirium pursues him. His youth, however, battles successfully against the fever that is consuming him. His weakness, and the derangement of his thoughts, gradually distancing themselves from a deadly memory, return him to a life that nearly escaped him. He is deaf to all consolation, though.

In vain, he is told about his colonel—who, told of his misfortune, has given him leave and freed him from his pledge to Scotland, which an unknown hand caused him to sign. Far from calming him, the generosity of the leader who had protected him reminds him of the stranger's treason. All his fury reviving, he shouts loudly for his weapons; he tries to get up, to fight a shadow that he thinks he can see in front of him.

A profound exhaustion immediately follows these impulses of a heart that no longer knows itself. Finally, time brings a calmness that becomes more favorable every day to the reason that is recovering its empire.

With health, Léonti finds a new energy. He wants to live in order to avenge his lover; the first desire he expresses is to see the wood, simultaneously so dear and so terrible, again. He drags himself to it, and everything there excites him, enchants him and drives him to despair.

It is there, at the foot of that solitary tree, that he received Bettina's first oaths; that her trembling hand squeezed his; that he swore in his turn to love no one but her; and that a kiss given by love and received by innocence, sealed the secret promise of their marriage—but alas, these trees, these shelters, discreet witnesses to the sweetest mysteries, have also played host to the efforts of crime. It is there too that Bettina, the victim of an abominable monster, perished in the flower of her youth!

What intoxicating memories, what frightful regrets, the same locations recall! Oh, how violently his heart beats! He comes and goes, stops, re-examines, strides forth—and, bewildered and beside himself, finally arrives at the extremity of the wood.

But then, what a spectacle strikes his eyes!

He sees a man sitting there, silhouetted against the places in front of him. This man, the clothes he wears, everything about him reminds him of the perfidious stranger, Bettina's murderer.

Léonti falls upon him with lightning rapidity, raising his arm to strike…

The stranger turns round. His face is unfamiliar; his eyes are moist with tears. Weeping, he looks at Léonti, whose wrath gives way to the compassion that grips him involuntarily.

"Young stranger," he says, in an emotional voice, "Forgive me. The state in which I see you dissipates an error to which your presence initially gave rise in my soul, tormented by a frightful dolor."

"Ah!" the stranger replies. "You're unhappy, as am I. Sit down beside me, and we shall both soften the bitterness of our regrets by telling one another our troubles."

Léonti feels the need to listen to a heart responsive to his own, and already, drawn together by an indefinable sympathy, they are yielding to the effusions of a consoling friendship.

When men born under the same skies, but adrift in foreign lands, who have never met before, encounter one another by chance so far from their paternal fields, a sudden emotion brings them together. The mannerisms, the clothing and the language of their fatherland makes them quiver, and each of them thinks that he has found a brother, a friend, a companion of his youth. In this way, a rapid interest unites two hearts crushed by misfortune.

Léonti, persuaded to speak first, relates the story of his love, so faithful and so unfortunate: his departure; his return to Venice; his dreads; his hopes; the stranger's perfidy; and Bettina's death.

At this final revelation of his story, his friend interrupts him with a cry that echoes in the distance.

"It's him!"

"What! You know him?"

"He's the author of all my misfortunes. Come, let's run after him. You know all of our enemy's crimes. Let's not risk losing precious time, and join forces to avenge ourselves."

"But, please explain!"

"Come on, I tell you, entrust yourself to a devoted friend. Let's go, without further delay."

This said, he forces Léonti to follow him.

A favorable wind pushes the boat that carries them, and soon, superb Venice, shrinking before their eyes, no longer presents itself as anything but a distant fugitive dot, which finally sinks into the water.

Part Two
The Pursuit of Lord Ruthwen

I

Lord Ruthwen, the mysterious man who hid his dreadful secret beneath the perfidious appearances of an amiability full of charm, had profited from an imperious opportunity to extract from the unfortunate Aubrey, his imprudent travelling companion, an oath to be silent for a year and a day regarding the crimes of which he had been the witness.

One recalls with terror that fatal oath, whose extraordinary empire enchained all of Aubrey's faculties, at the very moment when his sister, affianced to Lord Ruthwen in spite of him, became the victim of a silence that a supernatural power and the violence of his illness caused him to keep until the end.

Finally, destiny, which presides over everything and counts our moments, completed the union of all that the world offers of the most virtuous and most amiable with the sum of the most perverse and the most odious, and the day of the marriage, that primal day, so pure and sweet, the deceptive presage of a happiness that is believed to be eternal and which is of such short duration, that day full of life, was the unfortunate Georgina's tomb.

An extreme dolor had robbed Aubrey of the use of his senses for some time. The fear of those around him spread the news of his death everywhere, and yet, by an effort of nature, after a long lethargy, his pulse revived, his eyes opened, and the beating of his heart announced his return to life.

Vengeance was the first need that he experienced.

Scarcely back on his feet, he leaves London and launches himself on Lord Ruthwen's trail. He knows that the beautiful climate of Italy is the object of the desires and the goal of the travels of men to whom fortune permits these voluntary emigrations. A secret inspiration directs his search toward those smiling lands that he had already travelled in happier times.

He disembarks in Venice, and asks everywhere if anyone has seen him, if anyone knows Lord Ruthwen. Vain efforts! He can discover nothing. Then melancholy draws him to the shore of the Adriatic, and there, filled with a dolorous memory, inspired by the enchanting places that he admires, he inscribes on a piece of paper bathed with his tears the names of the places where he would like to be able to spend the rest of his life, with the beloved sister he will mourn forever.

It is in that situation that Léonti finds the inconsolable Aubrey. Their hearts understand one another at the first whimper of a dolor that has the same source. They leave, animated by the same sentiments, swearing never to part again.

Léonti's heart is too dolorously affected, however, and the loss he had just suffered is too recent to find relief in the distractions of the voyage. His sobs, his stifled sighs and his profound reveries all reveal the sickness tormenting him, and when his long-contained grief bursts forth with greater violence for the very effort he makes to hide it, Aubrey takes him in his arms, consoles him and weeps with him, and it is by sharing his troubles that he softens their bitterness.

When they left the Lido, the gondolier charged with carrying them to the next shore gazed at Léonti for a long time without daring to speak to him, but the grief of Bettina's lover made such a deep impression on him that, more than once, his hand released the oar, confiding the care of his vessel to the motionless sea. Finally, weary of maintaining silence, he said: "Léonti, all Venetians have mourned your misfortune. You deserve a better fate. Having served your fatherland, you ought to find recompense on our shores for the perils of war. Like you, I have served the standard of Venice, I have braved enemy fire, I have fought on the plain of Olmutz."[12]

"On the plain of Olmutz?" said Léonti.

"Yes," Nadoli continued, "and it was there, surrounded by enemies, that I was about to perish. Suddenly, a soldier arrived, saw my danger, and raced to my rescue."

"What are you saying? Speak—who was that soldier?"

"He wore the costume of our region, and when he appeared, he was alone."

"Alone?"

"By night."

"By night?"

---

[12] As the text will eventually specify, Olmutz (the German spelling of Olomouc) was the capital of Moravia, nowadays one of the Czech Republics. It is not obvious why Venetian troops would have been fighting there at the time when the story is set—which will also be specified eventually, although Bérard might not have had that date in mind at this stage of his story, given that it seems inconsistent with the temporal setting of the Polidori story to which this one is a sequel.

"And, as quick as lightning, his first action was to stop the blade that was about to strike me and kill the enemy who was menacing me."

"What's that?"

"Do you know that generous mortal? Is he dead, a victim of his own courage?"

"He lives—he is still breathing."

"Who is he?"

"It was me."

"O Heaven! What—that young soldier who, without knowing me, risked his life to save mine…"

"Was me."

"Who was immediately pursued, overwhelmed…"

"It was me!" Léonti repeated.

"Whom I attempted, unsuccessfully, to rescue…"

"It was me, I tell you!"

"And who, in his turn, struck by a mortal blow, fell dying at my feet?"

"It was me, in person."

"What about the wound he received?"

"Here it is!" said Léonti, explosively, uncovering his breast.

"Great God!" cried Nadoli, "It was you, Léonti?" And he fell at the feet of his rescuer.

Léonti lifted him up and hugged him in his arms. "Nadoli," he said, "since the death of Torelli's daughter, this is the first instant of consolation that I have found, perhaps the only one for which it was permissible for me to hope. Be happy in the places, ever loved and ever regretted, that I am leaving forever. I shall perish under a foreign sky. That is what destiny requires, which destroys the vain projects of human beings at its whim. Goodbye, then! Goodbye forever!"

At that moment, the vessel reached the shore. It was necessary to part.

Nadoli wanted to go with his savior. "Dispose of my life," he said, dissolving in tears. "Take it—it's yours."

Léonti did not have the strength to reply. He received the other's embraces, forbade him to follow him, and drew away—but in a voice interrupted by heart-rending sobs, in that tone which is so true and expressive that it produces a rapid and irresistible effect, with that cry from the heart whose vibration makes an immediate penetrating impact, resounds with so much force in the hearts of others, Nadoli still persisted.

"Friend! My benefactor! You to whom I owe my life, may Heaven preserve yours! Léonti! Farewell! Farewell!"

And the sea breeze continued to carry that farewell to Léonti, who was already far away.

II

Aubrey shakes his friend's hand sympathetically; the latter, able to understand that mute statement, replies with a tear. Nothing is purer, more consoling, than the memory of a generous action. For the benefactor, there is perhaps a reward greater than the benefit itself, which is the delightful emotion that it leaves behind.

They are soon far from the estates of Venice, however. Pursuing an enemy who always escapes them, they pass through many countries without pause.

In a happy situation, everything takes on a pleasing color for our observing eyes. We contemplate the inexhaustible beauties of nature ecstatically. A picturesque location, the slope of a hill, the summit of a mountain, the pure air one breathes there, an avalanche suspended over a precipice, an open space prolonged in a fleecy wood, a distant perspective fading away, the sun that, by virtue of a magical opposition, covers all the objects that interrupt its rays with a thousand shades of gold and azure, and darkens the shadows adjacent to its floods of light—all these scenes, which an immortal hand has placed in profusion in favorite climates, possess an admirable harmony that reanimates the delirium of poets, the inspiration of painters and the idle curiosity of travelers. But a man pursued by misfortune seems an exile on earth; the faculties of his imagination weaken. When his soul suffers, everything around him is sad. Respiring nothing but dolor, he obtains nothing from life save sensations whose diminished compass rends him insensible to everything that reproduces the distractions he rejects.

Such were the sentiments of Léonti and his friend. The marvels of nature had no attraction for them. If hazard led their path to a naïve scene of village love—a noisy troop of joyful harvesters, young men celebrating their return from labor and young women dancing in the green meadow to the music of guitars and amorous voices—far from pleasing Léonti, the variety of those happy groups, inspiring in their turn the gaiety that they inspired, further increased his sadness.

Aubrey, however, was impatient to go to Florence, where he was expected by a Neapolitan banker he had met during his earlier travels. Only a few leagues distant from that city, they were both hastening their pace in order to arrive there when a singular adventure forced them to stop at the first village through which they passed.

As they were approaching Roveredo their eyes were struck by bright light. The night was well advanced; the village, illuminated at all points by torches placed at close intervals, was dressed for a fête, and yet everything was dismal and silent; no singing could be heard.

That absence of melody, in a country where it seemed to be renewed at every step, was not a fortunate omen. Aubrey and Léonti went forward without daring to confide to one another the reason for their astonishment. As they entered the village, which seemed deserted at first, a cry of alarm emerged from a high window.

"There are two of them!" cried a voice—and these words, repeated, spread fear everywhere.

Long moans reply to them.

Aubrey stops, and tries to understand what might have caused the terror that their presence inspires. Léonti knocks at the door of a house that is more prominent than the rest. It does not open.

After further attempts to get in, he reverts to pleading. "We are two distraught travelers, whom misfortune has condemned to a voluntary exile. Grant us shelter for the night beneath your hospitable roof. Venice is my fatherland, and if storm winds cast your ship upon our shore, our urgent help would save you from the wreck. Why are you manifesting less generosity than us? Inhabitant of Roveredo, open your door to us."

After a long silence, someone appears at the window, and replies, in an uncertain voice: "Alas, take pity on us. One sole vampire suffices to put the whole village in turmoil, and there are two of you. Go away, or our wives and daughters will die of fright on seeing you."

"Vampires, us!" cries Aubrey, in astonishment. "You're mistaken. Far from resembling such monsters, we are in horror of them, as you are, and it's to liberate the earth from one of them that we have directed our path this way."

On this assurance, Rodogni hastens to come down and let them into his dwelling. In a vast, elegantly-decorated apartment, women gathered there tremble at the arrival of the two travelers, but soon, reassured by what the newcomers say, they recover from their fright, and Rodogni, yielding to Aubrey's entreaties, recounts the reason for their alarm.

"Two days ago," he says, "a vampire appeared in the village."

"Was he a foreigner?" asks Léonti.

"No," their host replies, "he was a native of this country. We knew him, and this is his story:

"Roberti, a poor farmer of the village, was the tenant of a domain that belonged to a rich Florentine. A poor harvest ruined him. He left for Florence and asked for help, which was refused. Forced to pay what he owed without delay, misery caused his health to deteriorate. When adversity weighs upon us, it seems that it overwhelms us with various disgraces at the same time, taking pleasure in draining the cup of bitterness to the dregs.

"In Roberti's absence, the modest field that his foreforefathers had worked was sold; his beloved wife died of grief, and a daughter, his sole consolation, was carried off by a foreign soldier. Driven to despair by so much misfortune, he came to request from his native soil a second helping of the wealth that was irredeemably lost, but found nothing but futile regrets. Fever took hold of him; his illness grew worse, and it did not take long to lead him to the grave.

"At this point, a prodigy commenced that still confounds me. Three days ago, Roberti was carried to the last resting-place of mortals, and the earth was already open to received him, when he leapt from his coffin, alive, and disappeared over our fields. At that unexpected apparition, the frightened priests covered their faces, the holy crucifix slipped from their hands, the religious torches went out, and the terrified women ran to spread the incredible news.

"That miraculous event gave rise to a thousand conjectures. Everyone knows that an incident much slighter than that one, unnoticed in a great city, rapidly acquires great importance in a village. In this remarkable circumstance, in my capacity as the local *podesta*,[13] I as-

---

[13] A *podesta* is a local official roughly equivalent to a French *maire*; like the latter term, it's precise significance evolved along with changing patterns of administrative organization.

sembled the resident elite and, after having consulted the savants of all centuries and all places by way of my books, it was decided, with unanimous agreement, that Roberti, suddenly returned to life, was a vampire, whose return it was necessary to anticipate.

"The danger was imminent. He had been seen roaming around the neighborhood. I gave orders. The men were armed, the women ran to the church, where public prayers were said, but the precautions were in vain, alas. Yesterday, at ten o'clock in the evening, the vampire ran through the village. His passage has chilled everyone's courage, and at this moment, we're waiting tremulously for the fatal hour to chime."

Indeed, scarcely has Rodogni pronounced these words than a great tumult becomes audible outside, cries coming from all directions. Léonti and Aubrey, hidden on the threshold of the podesta's house, precipitate themselves after a phantom that flees before them. Then, however, the mysterious man stops, throwing off the black cloak that had covered him, and renders them motionless with surprise by responding to their threats with repeated bursts of immoderate laughter.

They hasten to take the pretended vampire to Rodogni's house, where, as soon as he comes in, everyone cries: "It's Antonio! That madman Antonio!"

From that moment on, fear gave way to the most lively gaiety.

The two travelers were unable to understand anything of what was happening around them. They demanded an explanation from Antonio himself, who

---

There is no precise English equivalent, although the local squire would probably have held a vaguely similar position in the era in which the story appears to be set.

promised to tell the story of his vampirism, and began thus:

"Everyone acquires in being born a character that ordinarily accords with his physiognomy. Mine is not sad, and I am even cheerful to the point of madness. It was assuredly to punish me that I was imprisoned in an accursed place where I only found people who became furious when I spoke and who wept when I laughed. They're insane, I know, and I pity them—but at the end of the day, their society was not to my taste.

"My prison displeased me to such an extent that, surprisingly enough, I began to become serious. I felt that if I became bored, I was doomed, and I looked out for a favorable opportunity to save myself. It presented itself. They had forgotten to close a secret exit. I noticed it, and left—and here I am, free. But that wasn't the end of the matter. Once my escape was discovered, people would set out in my pursuit.

"What shall I do? I abandon myself to my star, which always guides me marvelously. I run toward this village. I encounter a chapel on my route. It is open. I go in. I was alone. I approach the altar, and in a coffin, which I am curious enough to open, I recognize…guess who? My friend Roberti. He was a good man, and I'm pleased to see him again—but while I'm looking at him, I hear noises at the chapel door, and make out torches. They're coming to fetch Roberti.

"My embarrassment is extreme. How can I get out without being seen? Fortunately, a mind like mine is fertile in expedients. An idea occurs to me, unique, singular and charming. I slide on top of the poor dead man and, thus hidden, allow myself to be carried away with him. You'll understand, however, that I have no desire to have myself buried alive.

"So, having arrived at the burial-ground, the funeral procession stops and deposits me on the ground; immediately, I say farewell to my friend, reach out my arms, take possession of his covering, stand up, and, as quick as lightning, escape through the crowd.

"Apparently, the people around me thought that the dead man had returned from the other world, for it was necessary to see them grow pale, turn their eyes away, utter screams and run away at top speed—truly, nothing could be funnier.

"The adventure was too amusing for me not to take pleasure in seeing it through to the end, and my plan was to come back every evening at the same time, to frighten the good souls of the village, who have courage, as you know, and have taken me for I don't know what. I was making my second nocturnal run when you stopped me. After that, let them say that I'm mad. You've heard me, and seen me—judge for yourselves."

Thus spoke Antonio. His return and his madness were soon known to all the inhabitants of Roveredo, and that ludicrous object of general terror then became an inexhaustible subject of merriment. He was taken back, by winding paths, to the accompaniment of musical instruments, to the place from which he had fled. Eulogies were delivered to the courage of the travelers who, more fatigued than satisfied by the adventure, got up at daybreak the following day and took the road to Florence again.

III

In the city, Aubrey found the Neapolitan banker to whom he had written, explaining the reason for his journey to Italy. The banker's name was Alberti. He made manifest to Aubrey the great pleasure that he obtained in seeing him again, and welcomed Léonti with the abandon, always so pleasurable, of an amity fortunate to be felt from the outset. He forced them to accept shelter in the house in which he was living, and there he said to Aubrey:

"I'm leaving for Naples tonight, on urgent business. The unfortunate Palmire, the daughter of Ganem Ali, a merchant from Bassora, who was entrusted to my care died yesterday in Florence. A few days ago, I still hoped to save her life, and even to make her happy. It was with that in mind that an English lord whom I met here, and whom I once saw with you, has gone to Naples to bring back the lover that she adored. Now that voyage is unnecessary, and I hope to arrive in time to prevent Lord Ruthwen from undertaking it."

At the name of Lord Ruthwen a sudden pallor covered Aubrey's face. Alberti perceived his agitation and asked him the reason for it. When learned of all the odious vampire's crimes, he urged the two friends to go with him of his own accord. Indeed, all three of them were animated by such a desire to lay their hands on the abominable Ruthwen that they traveled with extreme rapidity.

As soon as they arrived in Naples they carried out the most active search in all directions, but it was futile. No one had seen the man they described anywhere.

Alberti no longer had any doubt that Palmire had increased the number of the monster's victims, who brought despair and death everywhere he went, and always escaped human vengeance by flight. Aubrey and Léonti desiring to know what had befallen the young woman from Jerusalem, he promised to tell them the story in his summer residence, to which he invited them.

They had already passed through the city and reached the sea shore when an extraordinary scene attracted their attention. A young woman was being pursued by the people, and a boatman who had accompanied her was assuring everyone that she was a sorceress, of whom it was necessary to beware. He was complaining of not having received the price agreed between them for the journey.

Aubrey asked what he was owed and paid him. At the same time, confused cries announced that the pursuit was continuing. Léonti ran to protect the foreign woman; her clothing was reminiscent of the young women of Venice, and her pallor was extreme.

He launches himself forward, parts the crowd, and swears that he will defend her if there is any further insult to her misfortune. But what a surprise he has when, hearing a voice pronounce his name, he turns round and thinks he recognizes, in the young woman who is the object of the pursuit…

Great God! Bettina!

He calls to her, and runs after her—but the crowd has come between them, and she has disappeared.

Astonished by his confusion and distress, the people surround him, pressing upon him and interrogating him. Believing him to be in danger, Aubrey comes running, takes hold of him, and drags him away to a place where they can eventually converse in safety.

Léonti believes that he can still see the phantom that appeared to his eyes. "Yes, I saw her," he says. "It was really her!"

Aubrey, who is familiar with the causes of mental disorder, tries in vain to reassure him and attribute his fright to the delirium of a preoccupied imagination. Léonti persists in maintaining that he has seen Bettina. He wants to talk to the boatman.

"Where is he? Where does he come from? Has he come from Venice?"

To calm Léonti down, Aubrey sends people to search for the boatman, but he is not found; all that is learned is that the man, either by virtue of malice or superstition, had said that the young woman, having been dead for a brief interval, had returned to life and had set out in pursuit of her lover.

Aubrey smiles at the boatman's tale. He thinks he understands now why the people, whose credulity avidly adopts anything that is marvelous, had chased the young woman. He regrets not having seen her, in order to rescue her. "She's doubtless and unfortunate woman, prey to poverty," he adds, "or perhaps a victim of seduction and love."

Alberti confirms this opinion, with explanations that pique the curiosity of the two friends sharply.

"Almost all the inhabitants of our region," he says, "have a disorderly excitement in their ideas that makes them prefer the strongest emotion to the calm of rationality. Here, the head and the heart act with equal rapidity, and the sharper sentiments stifle belated reflection. The people are more turbulent and less civilized than anywhere else. They have all the faults that seem intrinsic to southern climes without possessing the qualities that temper their effervescence. They seek arousal, no

73

matter by what means, and it's that need for continual agitation which inspires such a keen appetite for extraordinary events. I'm convinced that the entire scene about which we're talking has no other cause than a touching story that is well-known in Naples. It's the story of the white woman, which I shall tell you:

The Story of the White Woman

A Neapolitan lord, exiled from court by a sudden disgrace, had retired to a château some distance from the city. There, in isolation, forgetting vain worldly pleasures and the people who had done him an injustice, he brought up a son, the sole heir to his illustrious name and vast fortune.

To begin with, young Mancini divided his time between study and rural amusements, but soon, having reached an age at which the imagination becomes excited, the blood seethes, and the heart leaps and sinks in response to sensations for which it is avid, his ideas took a new direction. A vague desire for change led him to prefer hunting to other, less active, pleasures. He left the château every day at first light, fleeing an ennui that followed him everywhere, and was driven thus to the most distant fields.

It was during one of these excursions that he encountered a young woman of striking beauty. Maria had the simplicity and rural freshness that is the charming adornment of a shepherdess in the flower of youth. Her embarrassment, the uncertainty of her gait, the sound or her voice, and her anxiety on seeing Mancini, all gave her a grace more piquant than her beauty. Even her flaws made her more attractive. Such is nature; she is inimitable. The art that seeks to surprise her always goes over her head; ornamentation veils her secret, and one destroys her charm in seeking to embellish it.

The amorous Mancini was no longer alive, save when he was with Maria. He obtained her permission to see her, to talk to her and to listen to her every day, at agreed times. These times, always too long delayed, became Mancini's entire life. With what impatience the beating of his heart echoed the ticking of the clock that anticipated them!

Who has not known the violence of first love, and the intoxicating illusion of a happiness whose outcome, often distant and sometimes inaccessible, always seems so imminent? Alas, that happiness, whose disturbance is so sweet, is no longer recoverable in the storm of passions, the inconstancy that follows them and the frightful emptiness that they leave behind; like a distant impression that never leaves us, however, its sweet memory consoles our entire lives.

Mancini effortlessly seduced a simple heart open to love. Maria became a mother, and from then on, her lover was everything to her. She saw in him her first friend and last refuge. Poor Maria! She did not know that happiness flies far away from a woman who has given everything to love, at the very moment when it seems forever fixed beside her.

Mancini's father, however, anxious about his son's morning excursions and the change in his temperament, had him followed and his every step watched. He soon knew the secret of his love-affair with Maria. Alarmed by a liaison that was contrary to all his views, he hastened to remove his son from the dangerous solitude that had doomed him.

Taken to Naples, Mancini was initially watched so closely that he could not get away for a single day to see the victim of his seduction. Surrounded by distractions and fêtes, avid for pleasures that were new to him, he forgot Maria, and only a few months had gone by since his departure from the château when his marriage was arranged to the daughter of Duc Orlandi.

While the ingrate Mancini was entirely devoted to his new wife, what became of the unfortunate Maria? Astonished at no longer seeing him, she did not know how to explain his absence, but the heart is quick to forgive the object of its love; it exhausts all appearances and all flattering errors before believing it to be guilty.

Finally, a disquiet that grows by the hour illuminates and destroys ever-deceptive hope. No longer able to resist her pain, Maria goes in search of her lover. Her maternal tenderness awakens, already giving her the strength to withstand anything. She conceives the stratagem of introducing herself to the château without letting it be known what has brought her there.

She knocks. "Open up," she says. "Open up! I'm lost…unfortunate."

She hears nothing. Are the doors of the rich so difficult to open to the tears of the pleading poor?

She knocks again. The same silence. "What!" she continues, with a dolorous sigh. "Is there no one in the château who recognizes my voice and will respond? Open up! It's a little bread that I'm asking for—take pity on my poverty!"

Vain hope! Her touching plea dies away around her, and no one seems to have heard it.

In fact, the château was deserted. Maria did not know that.

She does not call out again. Mute now, her heart heavy with sighs, she goes away, weeping.

The next day, she returns, as night approaches. "This time," she says, "he will hear me; sleep has not yet rendered him insensible to my cries. Sleep! Can he sleep while I suffer, while I am close by, asking for him, call-ing to him in the name of the child of our love? No, he will hear me. May my song reach him with a reproach that I would be only too happy to forget in his arms. Let's try."

So saying, according to the habit of the region, she picks up the guitar suspended from her shoulder, and, tremulously, sings the melancholy refrain f a ballad that Mancini had taught her.

In the place where I lived in peace,
When the seducer set his stall,
I often, on my discreet fleece,
Repeated his flattering call.
He said: if a love that's entire
Gives rise to a thrill of delight,
A desire not matched by desire,
Is the source of a terrible blight.

At the sentiment newly laid bare,
My heart, swiftly eager to bloom,
Still young, was as yet unaware
That love might be coupled with gloom.
Alas, I found out on my own
That love does not always shine bright.
While my love persists, his has flown!
And the source of a terrible blight.

Already tremulous, cast out,
I must and dare not flee this place;
My sore heart is oppressed by doubt
And tears are flowing down my face.
He has abandoned me to pain!
Mortal, Mancini, is my plight,

To die without seeing my love again
Is the source of a terrible blight!

Her guitar ceased to vibrate. The profoundest silence reigned around her.

She listens again, and, her foot suspended, holds her breath. All is silent. No more hope. She falls, her guitar hits the ground, breaks, and echoes in the distance like a groan fading away in space.

Attracted by the noise, a stranger came running. He had come down from his carriage. It seemed that his assistance was futile. On arriving in Naples, he was told that Maria was dead.

That news spread rapidly through the city; it was the sole topic of conversation. Mancini unveiled its mystery. He ran in search of Maria, saw her lying at the foot of a tree, inundated her with his tears, and tried to recall her to life.

Belated promises! Superfluous efforts! His lover is lost to him.

In despair, by virtue of his culpable neglect and its cruel consequences, he did not hesitate to confide his keen anguish and remorse to a spouse worthy of him. Emilia consoled him, approved his decision to live in the château from which his father had removed him, to Maria's misfortune, and went with him, pronouncing these touching words:

"Weep for your lover, Mancini. Weep for her always. Your attachment, your belated but generous regret, moves me to greater affection. Love me as you love her. Have your child brought, and I shall teach him to cherish you. He is a stranger to our love, but I shall always have a smile for him."

Since then, they have lived at the château—and it is said that every year, on the same day, at the same hour, a white woman appears by night. When ten o'clock chimes, knocking is heard at the door. More than once, someone has tried to discover the secret of that mysterious apparition, but, by virtue of a bizarrerie that remains inexplicable, when all the people in the chateau, placed on different sides, watch out for the phantom's arrival, they hear knocking, but never see anyone—and the door quivers several times, without anyone being able to make out the cause.

A thousand rumors have run around concerning that extraordinary adventure. Some claim to have recognized Maria, others to have heard her asking for her child. Credulity, which feeds on chimeras, has rendered that version popular, and it is because of that memory that the young woman who appeared this morning in the public square caught the general attention.

Such is the story of the white woman.

The Pursuit of Lord Ruthwen
(continued)

IV

"The story of Maria, which links genuine misfortunes to scarcely-credible events," said Aubrey, "reminds me of another adventure that happened in Moravia. People worthy of trust have assured me that a young Moravian woman, betrayed by her lover, returned after her death to pursue him everywhere. If one can believe everything that is recounted, that would be the first example of a female vampire."

"Ah!" said Léonti, struck by what he had just heard. "If an incredible hazard has returned Bettina to life, it must be to reunite herself with me, to protect me and to put an end to my torments that she is following in my footsteps."

"I can see," his friend said to him, taking him in his arms, "that the scene we witnessed this morning is still tormenting your thoughts. That distressing image bore too close a relationship to your misfortunes. We must leave this place, which maintains painful memories. We'll leave for Rome tomorrow. There, masterpieces of art and an inspirational environment will astonish our imagination, and perhaps restore a necessary calm to our distress."

The following day they said farewell to Alberti, who made vain efforts to retain them.

During the journey, Léonti abandoned himself silently to his sad reveries. For a long time, Aubrey could not distract him therefrom. Finally, by the lure of a conversation that was both compassionate and witty, he brought to his friend's eyes a gleam of that hope which the unfortunate never lose, and succeeded in mingling a few gentle consolations with his sadness.

What power a true friend has over us, by virtue of his generous concern, his pleasant discourse, his honest emotion and the abandon which is its surest testimony! His persuasive eloquence penetrates to the depths of heart, doubles the joys that it experiences, ameliorates the pain that it shares, embellishing both—and that voice, always so dear, often lost to love, is never lost to friendship.

There was talk in Rome just then of a young Arab whom misfortunes unknown to everyone had exiled from his homeland. Nothing brings men together more than a conformity of character or situation. Aubrey and Léonti sought out Nadoor Ali. Chance brought them to share the same dwelling.

Accustomed to seeing one another, and wanting to be together, they formed a liaison that grew closer by the day, and soon, fleeing the unwelcome gaiety of all the travelers that curiosity of the study of the fine arts attract to the immortal city, they finally formed a permanent company.

Nadoor Ali was in the full bloom of youth; he had a noble bearing and a handsome face, and his stern expression, his tanned complexion and his sparkling eyes gave his entire physiognomy a remarkable character. His new friends did not take long to perceive that, like them, he was nursing the memory of a great misfortune.

Mutual confidences succeeded vague conversations of little interest. Once confidence was established, their tears flowed over the misfortunes of a love reduced to despair by the loss of an adored object, and soon a sigh, uttered by Léonti and repeated by Aubrey, interrogated the dolor of Nadoor Ali. He spoke about a young Greek woman, captive in Arabia, and promised to tell the story of her misfortunes.

A few days passed without the Arab seeming disposed to satisfy their curiosity, although his sadness had increased.

One day, while they were examining the masterpieces that were Michelangelo's legacy to the admiration of the centuries, they noticed a Roman woman in the crowd whose clothing advertised the opulence of an elevated status. The lady's eyes were fixed upon Nadoor Ali, and she never ceased looking at him. Aubrey noticed it, but what astonished him more was Nadoor Ali's indifference, his attention being entirely devoted to the admirable ornaments decorating a ceiling, all of which had been animated by the breath of genius.

The hour was late, though, and it was necessary to leave. The unknown woman, who was following them with her eyes, made a gesture, gave an order to a servant, and climbed up into a shiny litter. The procession drew away. The incident made Aubrey think that Nadoor Ali had some amorous intrigue in progress in Rome, but, not wanting to penetrate a secret that did not belong to him, he did not share his observations with anyone else.

Rome is full of superb monuments, but, surrounded only by a few historically celebrated mountains, its outskirts offer few shady places where the heat of the day may be avoided. In that hot climate, the moment when the cool of a fine evening begins is impatiently awaited. Immediately it declares itself, the countryside is covered with elegant costumes, and in the city, the artisan seated on the threshold of his dwelling, glad to escape his customary toil,[14] celebrates in melodious song the pure air that he breathes and the joy of living beneath the beautiful Italian sky.

O evening hour so dear to lovers, whose return has been hastened by desire, whose pleasures are sung by discreet voices!

After wandering on the Palatine Hill, the three friends direct their stroll toward the gilded waves of the Tiber. Halted on the illustrious banks by so many ancient memories, they contemplate the distant effects of the Sun, which, now only coloring the Earth feebly, still strikes the water with its dying fire, and seems to be disappearing regretfully as the shades of night approach.

Nadoor Ali is inspired by this imposing spectacle. "O Cymodora!" he cries. "I believe that I see you still amid the ruins of Athens, tuning your sonorous lyre to the roaring waves of the sea!"

This said, he stops, confused by having betrayed his secret in pronouncing the charming name of Cymodora.

Aubrey gazes at him compassionately, and with a touching plea invites him to pour out his desolate heart into the bosom of amity.

Nadoor Ali seems momentarily indecisive; then, sitting down between them, he wipes away a tear trickling down his cheek. He is about to speak, and Aubrey and Léonti are already lending him attentive ears, when they are interrupted by the rapid arrival of a charger, which sends a cloud of dust flying up before them.

A slave hands a letter to Nadoor Ali and, without saying a single word, spurs the flanks of his agile mount

---

[14] Bérard inserts a footnote here: "*Dolce far niente.*" [Sweet idleness.]

again—which, taking the road back to Rome, soon disappears from view.

Nadoor Ali is quick to consult his friends about the letter he has just received.

"It is necessary," he says, "that I tell you about my situation. It is embarrassing. Being more familiar with the customs of the country we are living in, perhaps you can give me some useful advice. I promise to follow it blindly; but before anything else, I owe you a few explanations regarding that which preceded today's event.

"I belong to one of the most celebrated families of the Orient. A terrible misfortune had exiled me from the shore of a homeland that I still regret. On my arrival in Rome, I was forced to yield to the insistences of the principal lords of the court of the Christian pontiff. I was present at fêtes from which might profound dolor ought to have banished me.

"At one of these numerous assemblies, surrounded by tumultuous pleasures, I became the object of universal curiosity, doubtless excited by my foreign appearance. A lady paid me flattering attentions. Hazard had placed me next to her. My sadness intrigued her. She interrogated me about my misfortunes. I seemed sensible to the testimony of her benevolence, but I avoided telling her secrets that I was obliged to keep. My reserve increased her desire to know me better. Before we parted, she pointed out her palace and exacted a promise from me that I would see her again.

"I was withdrawing from the noisy place where I had met her when a man came toward me and, in a fit of fury whose cause I found out too late, made it necessary for me to defend my life from his attack. I emerged victorious from the unfortunate duel. My attacker died in my arms, telling me that he was the lover of the Duchess d'A***.

"That adventure, whose consequences I deplored, fortified me even further in the decision I had made not to see the Roman woman again. The death of her lover made a great deal of noise at court. His family is powerful; it wanted to avenge him, but no one knew whose hand had struck him down, and the details that I had an interest in hiding. My safety was compromised. The slightest indiscretion would have doomed me. In order not to awaken my enemies' curiosity, I have lived since then in solitude, not confiding my grief and anxieties to anyone.

"I learned that the relatives of the nobleman who had succumbed to my blows were still making inquiries. Meanwhile, the Duchess—who had doubtless guessed the identity of the guilty party, far from naming me and delivering me to the pursuit of my enemies, has not ceased to give me proofs of a veritable interest. I do not know why, and can only think about everything that has happened to me. She was close to us yesterday, at the famous monument we visited, and this is what she has written to me…"

Nadoor Ali handed the letter to Aubrey then, who read it. It asked the young foreigner to go at a certain nocturnal hour to a certain place, from which a devoted messenger would take him to the palace, where he was expected.

The reading of this note gave rise to a lively debate between the three friends. Aubrey and Léonti asserted that the rendezvous, for which no reason was given, was a plot hatched by Nadoor Ali's enemies, and that, in a country where perfidy often sharpens the dagger of vengeance in the shadows, one would do better to consult prudence than a bravery surrounded by dangers devoid of honor.

"Oh well!" Nadoor Ali exclaimed, "If someone has designs on my life, I know how to defend myself against vile assassins."

"Friend," said Aubrey, "Yield to our wise advice, and leave to our experience the task of rendering the blows that are intended to strike you harmless. I shall go in your stead to tonight's rendezvous."

"No, said Léonti, "accustomed to the language of the country, I shall present myself on your behalf. I shall be able to thwart any criminal attempt."

"I cannot consent," The young Arab replied. "I cannot permit you to expose yourselves to dangers reserved for me."

The tone in which Nadoor Ali pronounces these words does not permit any further insistence on the generous offers that noble pride had made him refuse. Aubrey thus has recourse to trickery to protect him, in spite of himself, from the danger that threatened him. He obtains permission to accompany him.

An expressive glance makes Léonti understand that he is counting on him for the execution of a plan that they have to concoct without Nadoor Ali's knowledge.

V

Everything being thus arranged, they go to the determined spot that night. In accordance with a plan agreed with Aubrey, however, Léonti has preceded them. He arrives at the rendezvous first; alone, but armed, he has no fear, and, proud to be risking his life to save that of a friend, his courage is ready to brave the expected danger.

The hour chimes. A slave, enveloped in a large cloak, presents himself and whispers the name of Nadoor Ali. In response to that name, Léonti takes his hand and follows his guide, who opens a secret door, introduces him into a vast garden, and disappears.

Léonti advances through the somber clumps of trees. He listens; light footsteps seem to be coming from the side. He stops. A hand presses his; it is a woman's. Is this the presage of a mysterious joy? He reproaches himself then for having deprived his friend of a fortunate meeting in which his heart cannot take part. He allows himself to be led through thick foliage, discreetly confident of amorous pleasures that are about to be offered to him.

"O you," says a passionate voice, "whom my gaze has picked out, whom my heart has chosen, tell me whether yours is ready to share all that I have felt for you since he day I first saw you. Speak—say the word and I shall fly into your arms."

Léonti, forbidden this speech, does not know how to reply. Suddenly, a noise some distance away, like the rustle of a tunic, frightens he woman who has just spoke. She huddles against Léonti and, with a hand that she rapidly places over his mouth, bids him be silent. She dare not even breathe…

A dry leaf on the ground has rustled again. There is no more doubt; someone is walking stealthily. The person comes nearer, and a voice is heard close at hand.

"Léonti," it says. "Léonti! You're forgetting Bettina."

"Great God!" Léonti cries, beside himself. "What have I heard? It's her! It's her voice! Where are you, then, Bettina?"

At these imprudent exclamations, a sudden agitation is manifest in the palace. Torches circulate on all sides. Léonti, left alone, does not know which way to go. He searches for the path by which he has come, and finds the initial exit—but, just as he is about to make his escape, he is reached by armed slaves who fall upon him.

He defends himself furiously; Aubrey and Nadoor Ali run to his aid. Blood runs. Two men from the palace fall, lifeless.

A dazzling light appears in the distance, already illuminating the battleground. The three friends flee, without separating, ever ready to repel a further attack, returning home at a precipitate pace.

They confide their situation to the proven loyalty of their host, who hastens to serve them. He tells them that the Duchess A*** is the niece of the most powerful and most vindictive cardinal in the court of Rome.[15] His haughty character is well-known and feared. No one can

---

[15] It is not impossible that "niece" is meant literally, but it is probably significant that the ostensibly-celibate cardinals of the Vatican conventionally introduced their mistresses and catamites as "nieces" and "nephews."

hide for long from the pursuit of his authority. The slightest delay in fleeing will be fatal. He therefore urges them to leave, making the preparations himself, and darkness is still covering the Roman countryside with its somber veils when they take the road to the Duchy of Modena.

Their guide conducts them to the home of a friend of the generous Roman. They find a discreet hospitality there. In a house in the countryside, some distance from the city, an untroubled rest, embellished by the most assiduous care, soon dissipates their all-too-justified anxieties.

They did not realize at first, however, that Léonti had received a wound while defending himself. Nadoor Ali was the first to notice it. He offered Léonti the most affectionate reproaches, lavished the most urgent cares upon him, and made him promise not to go out until he was completely cured.

That adventure, in which they had run the same risks, made the bonds that already bound them together even tighter. Only Léonti seemed to conserve a memory that troubled his reason periodically.

Aubrey obtained a confession of these new anxieties. The apparition of Bettina in the palace garden pursued Léonti everywhere. He saw her by day, spoke to her by night. Nothing could dispel the idea that Bettina was alive, but the more he thought about it, the less he understood the impenetrable mystery. Finally, to clear up his doubts, he asked Aubrey to tell him the story of the young Moravian woman who had returned after her death to follow her lover everywhere.

"Calm down, dear Léonti," Aubrey replied, "I'll satisfy your curiosity. I still have the manuscript of the story you want to hear, and I'll read it to you:

The Story of the Young Moravian Woman

1

Moravia, which extends northwards as far as the fields of Bohemia and Silesia, is bordered on the southern side by the powerful Empire of which it is a tributary. Its fertile lands are irrigated by abundant waters whose springs escape the numerous mountains that traverse them, and which add their agrarian acreage to the rich agricultural terrains of the valleys—and the blue waves of the Morava flow through the superb Olmutz, the ancient capital of Moravia.

The celebrated family of Alberg, whose origins are lost in the night of time, shone with a merited brilliance in the first rank of the imperial nobility. The Albergs had been rendered famous by an uninterrupted sequence of outstanding services and glorious perils. Thus, proud of the rights acquired by the exploits that create heroes and the virtues that cause them to be cherished, they wished to transmit their long-historic name, pure and respected, through future ages. *Sacrifice life to honor* was their motto.

There remained of that illustrious house two brothers—who, being valiant in war, sustained the glory of their ancestors—and a young princess, a model of grace and beauty.

Elzine lived in the castle of her forefathers in Moravia. Some time before, her two brothers had come back to her, but, impatient to hear the call to battle, they longed for its imminent return. To forget the ennui of a time of rest they found difficult to tolerate, they hosted tournaments that brought together the elite of Moravian knighthood. Elzine did the honors of these festivals with that delightful generosity which, indulgent to all, welcoming to glowing happiness but more occupied with the suffering of the unfortunate, wins gratitude and does not allow complaint to make itself heard.

Already, though, Elzine is seeking solitude. Wearied by homages, alone with Athalise, her closest friend and the confidante of her most cherished secrets—the generous Athalise, whose devotion to her is absolute—Elzine releases the tears that must be hidden from the suspicious pride of her brothers.

Soon, war is declared. The order has arrived to leave without delay.

"Sister," says the younger Alberg, on departure, "Called, as we are, to sustain the honored name of our house, you must live in retreat during our absence. Do not permit any impure suspicion to arise as to the virtue of Elzine. Remember that, for a young beauty, honor is the flower of life. If Fate betrays the success of our arms, you will learn that our amity has foreseen everything and forgotten nothing. Farewell, Sister…"

"Farewell!" repeated one of Alberg's followers, a young cavalier, his voice low and his eyes moist with tears. "Farewell, Elzine! Think of our love and the unknown pledges, so dear, that I leave behind me."

They are already far away, and that discreet voice still echoes dolorously in Elzine's heart as she falls into the arms of her dear Athalise.

Taken to her apartment, Elzine wants to hide from all eyes. She forbids everyone to approach the isolated dwelling that she has chosen. There, her tears flow in abundance. She bathes her bed in them, and covers her friend's bosom with them. Athalise weeps with her, consoles her, and lavishes the most tender caresses upon her, but cannot restore calm to that tormented soul.

"Oh, Athalise, dear Athalise!" says Elzine, "I'm dying. You alone remain to me for support is the most cruel distress. What can I do? What will become of me? O Heaven, take pity on me!"

A fever breaks out. Her condition deteriorates. Midnight chimes. The part of the castle in which she resides is deserted. The darkness favors a bold plan.

Athalise leaves. Alone, without witnesses, she shivers in fear. Her foot trembles at the slightest rustle of the foliage that she brushes in the darkness, but perhaps, by means of her mysterious withdrawal, she might save her friend. A woman's heart, weak in its own suffering, is animated by a divine courage and a sublime devotion in the service of unhappy individuals whom she loves.

The day after that cruel night, Athalise does not appear at the castle at all. The anxious Elzine counts the hours and, the minutes. A thousand obstacles loom up in her sad thoughts. The happiness of her entire life, perhaps her life itself, depends on the dangerous secret of a step that everything obliges her to hide and that nothing must betray.

Finally, rapid familiar footfalls are heard. The door opens; it is Athalise. Her assured gaze and soft smile announce good news. She has succeeded.

Elzine hugs her affectionately for a long time, and her expressive silence speaks to her friend's heart.

A few months have gone by, however, and Elzine is lamenting having received no news of the army when a courier arrives at the castle in all haste and hands her a letter.

"Go back to Elzine's brothers," Athalise says to the messenger, "and tell them that their long silence and the dangers of war have alarmed her tenderness and brought her to the state in which you see her. Their prompt return would restore her health."

The messenger leaves. Elzine breaks the seal and reads, in a tremulous voice:

Dear Elzine,

Success has crowned our arms. We have lost warriors dear to our friendship, but a glorious peace is the prize of our exploits. We shall arrive at the castle tomorrow with the governor of Moravia, who wants to see you. Prepare to show him all the pleasure that the honor he accords to us causes us to experience.

Until tomorrow, Sister
Eric von Alberg

"Do you understand, Athalise? *We have lost warriors dear to our friendship*, my brother says. Here, read it—I'm trembling."

"Don't worry," says Athalise. "War harvest warriors, but Fate sometimes spares the life of the object of our dearest desires, and you should not yield to cruel alarms in advance."

"Oh," the princess replies, "How can I hide my distress from my brothers' eyes?"

"You must—be brave."

"And why is Prince Adalbert coming?"

"He wants to see you."

"To see me! What does he want? I don't know why, Athalise, but everything is frightening me and tormenting me."

The next day, the castle fills up with riders. A cavalry troop precedes the arrival of the governor. Elvine has mustered all her strength to hide her sadness and greet her brothers.

They arrive, and fly into Elzine's arms—but she searches for the eyes of a cavalier that she could not see. She dare not interrogate any of those around her.

"Brother," she finally says to Eric, "I've been in fear for your life. You've triumphed, and I thank Heaven for that, but if you're to be believed, your friendship has suffered costly losses."

"Yes, Sister," says Alberg, "victory often costs the victors more tears than the vanquished."

"What about Fernand, your companion in arms?"

"Alas!"

"He had saved your life in battle."

"He was my faithful friend; I regret his loss; I weep for him."

"He's dead!" says Elzine, leaning on Athalise for support.

"He died gloriously, with your name on his lips…he was so devoted to our family."

"Fernand is dead!" Elzine repeats, her voice faltering.

"Such is the destiny of arms," Alberg adds.

At that moment, the governor arrives.

"Sister," says Eric, "here is the prince." He addresses himself to the governor and adds: "Please excuse her—the dangers that we have run have drained her strength, and her affection for us renders her even dearer."

"And more beautiful," says Athalise, looking at Elzine. *gay*

Elzine retires to her apartments. Even her brothers,
alarmed by her pallor, demand that she avoids the fati-
gues of a fête. The governor watches her withdraw, regretfully, and expresses the sentiment so tenderly that
Elzine is troubled by it—but everyone is mistaken about
the reason for her emotion.

2

Elzine's fears were all too well-founded. Her brothers had been dreaming for a long time of providing her
with a husband worthy of her and their ambition. They
had spoken about it to their friend the prince, and his
visit to the castle had no other purpose.

Adalbert had often heard eulogies sung to Elzine.
As soon as he saw her, he found her beauty above its
renown, and that same day he declared his desire to marry her. The Albergs gave him their word, and immediately warned Elzine to prepare herself for a marriage
that would fulfill all their desires.

What reply could she make to brothers driven solely
by ambition? What resistance could she mount to desires
that were unshared, but which no obstacle could block?
What confession could she make?

Obedience was the only course remaining to Elzine;
with a heart heavy with regret and eyes filled with tears,
she pledged a heart lost to happiness at the altar.

Her extreme depression, on a day when everyone
ought to smile at her vows, however, troubled Adalbert's
love. Hastening to take her to his palace in Olmutz, he
was prodigal with all the pleasures of his court in order

to please Elzine—but nothing could distract her from her profound sadness.

The prince attributed this constant melancholy to the reserve of a young beauty brought up in solitude, and soon, happier with an adored wife, he obtained a son from her, who was named Oscar.

Athalise had gone with her friend, but the governor tried in vain to keep her at court. She always refused to leave a delightful house, not far from the city, in which she resided. It was in that charming retreat, embellished by Elzine's friendship, that Athalise lived happily, bringing up with extreme care a young girl named Thelemy, who always accompanied her on her visits to the palace.

Oscar and Thelemy were nearly the same age. They grew up and became handsome together. Oscar was lively and turbulent, but generous and quick to repair any harm that he did. Thelemy, always mild and affectionate, seemed resigned to suffering.

Thus innate character announces itself and develops within us.

In the midst of their games, vain pleasures of an age unknown to others and to itself, the young prince, born to command, already wanted to direct everything. At the slightest resistance he lost control and demolished the inconstant edifices that had cost their impatient hands so much effort, but an amiable sensitivity followed close on the heels of his anger. He would fly immediately into Thelemy's arms, embrace her, console her, and swear that he would be good henceforth, and obey her. Thelemy would weep and say, with a touching expression: "How unhappy I am!"

Alas, this childish cry, uttered in a grief as slight as the object that had produced it, would perhaps one day by the only one that her heart would be able to repeat.

Thus pass the early moments of life, scarcely felt, as quickly forgotten; thus fly those happy years when, so close to nascent passions and so far from the anticipation of their storms, one enjoys a tranquility that, soon lost, never returns, and which one always regrets.

Thelemy had reached the charming age at which everything seems beautiful to our eyes. Every spring caused more grace to blossom within her. The friendship, so naïve and so pure, that had bound her to Oscar thus far, was a sentiment that became more tender by the day, and the need to feel it had given rise to the desire to hide it.

For his part, Oscar, more timid in approaching Thelemy, could not account for the new anxiety that he was experiencing. Both of them were increasingly silent, and more reserved. Apart, they made a thousand plans with regard to everything to say to one another, but together, they dared not speak. Forced to see one another more rarely, they desired it more, and it was then that, escaping from the customary effusiveness of childhood, the delirious recklessness of the heart, they yielded innocently to all the charms of a danger still unknown but ready to explode.

A ball given at the court informed them that a tumultuous love had replaced their ingenuous confidence. Thelemy appeared there with all the attractions of youth, making no effort to please and pleasing everyone. She was the object of all desires, the subject of all flattering remarks. Beautiful without wanting to appear so, she danced as nimbly as a woodland shepherdess; her grace was delightful.

Oscar was moved and enchanted. At each cry of admiration she excited, he shivered visibly, and when Thelemy was praised, one might have thought that the praise was addressed to him, so much did it flatter his love. In the midst of the varied groups in which everyone delivered themselves to the pleasure of animated dancing, however, every time that a strange hand clasped the hand of his beloved, he went pale and red by turns—and if he tried to form some steps with her himself, the desire that he had to please her augmented his embarrassment.

Thus, perpetually agitated by the hoped of being loved by her, and even more by the dread of not being, the young and charming Oscar forgot all his advantages. He became the most timid of men, because he was the most amorous of them.

O trouble of the senses, delirium of the heart; vague desires, such sweet torments, the delights of first love—what pleasures are yours! It is then that life is no more than the most beautiful of dreams. Why can it not last forever?

Meanwhile, Athalise, whose health was deteriorating by the day, was too weak to come to the palace. Elzine often went to console and look after her.

The young prince is tormented by not seeing Thelemy. No longer able to resist his anxiety, he begs and pleads, and convinces his mother to send him to Athalise's house.

He soon traverses the distance separating him from his young friend. The first thing that he sees is Thelemy, occupied in embroidering a scarf. Nonplussed by his arrival, and unable to find words to express her surprise, she gets up anxiously—and that embarrassment, the indication of a love that is betraying itself, gives rise to suspicions in the jealous Oscar that he still dare not allow to burst forth. His gaze speaks for him, though.

After a momentary silence he says: "I can see that my presence is troubling you—I'm being indiscreet."

"Indiscreet!" says Thelemy. "You? Why?"

"That scarf…"

"What's the matter?"

"That charming scarf is for a cavalier?"

"Yes, Oscar, it's for a cavalier."

"He loves you?"

"I think so."

"And you love him?"

Thelemy remains silent, and sighs.

"Ah!" says Oscar, with a resentful gesture. "If only I'd known!"

"Stop, prince, and don't insult your friend. Wounding jealousy is a sentiment unworthy of both of us."

"Forgive me, forgive me, Thelemy! I dread not being loved by you."

"Oh, my God, do you hear him? He says that I do not love him! Can one ever forget one's first friend?"

"Your first friend—yes, that I am; but is friendship, dear Thelemy, still sufficient to our desires? Oh, I feel…"

"Speak."

"I love you like a sister!"

"I cherish you like a brother!"

"I'd like to see you all the time, at every moment, everywhere."

"I'd like that too."

"When I see you…"

"When you appear…"

"At first, my heart stops."

"Mine stops at the very sight of you; and then…"

"And then…it beats forcefully!"

"Dear Oscar!"

"Thelemy!"

A soft silence succeeds this animated scene, but the most tender confession is close to betraying them.

"Thelemy," Oscar continues, "I'm going away."

"You're leaving?"

"Tonight, for the army. My father commands it."

"O Heaven! For the army! You're going to risk the life that is so dear to me!"

"In three days I'll be able to come back to you."

"You promise?"

"I swear it."

"Oh well! Wait...take this scarf. I made it for you. Let it be your adornment. Look under this pleat—it's your name. Read it: *For Oscar*. That's the cavalier for whom it was destined."

"Ah!" says Oscar, enchanted. "Permit my joy..."

Thelemy escapes from his arms, crying: "Don't forget Thelemy."

"Me? Forget her? Never! Never!" the prince repeats to his beloved, who is already no longer able to hear him.

Proud to bear that cherished scarf, he thinks himself invincible. He runs precipitately, arrives at the palace, goes back and forth, returns a hundred times over to the places dear to his earliest memories. He roams the beloved woods of his childhood. He sees the ancient chapel in which his heart, virginal still, made the first oath of love; and the solitary spinney, the discreet shelter of a happiness without alarm; and the white rose, her favorite, the simple ornament of a bosom more charming than the flower that adorns it; and the hospitable tree whose inconstant bark changes, reproduces itself, changes again, and still conserves the imprint of his

amorous carving. Everything softens his heart, everything charms him, everything speaks to his excited soul.

Clad in his armor and decked with his scarf, however, he has had his father's orders; he has to leave for
the army. He leaves. Already, though, more impatient
for love than glory, he is dreaming about the moment of
his return.

3

Athalise does not get better. Thelemy answers an
order from Elzine, who wants to speak to her. She goes
into the vast gardens of the palace, and advances at a
slow pace through the places that were once so animated, but seem deserted now. Oscar is no longer there.
An involuntary charm draws her toward an orange tree,
her favorite, for which her young hands cared. Surprise!
A piece of paper is suspended from a branch. She runs
forward nimbly, grabs hold of the mysterious note,
opens it tremulously, and reads:

> *Love for her!*
> *To see her, to love her, to be loved by her,*
> *That is my desire.*
> *I think of her always, and everywhere.*
> *I love her so much! She is so beautiful*
> *That I repeat, night and day:*
> *Love for her!*
> *Love!*
>
> *Faithful friend,*
> *I always knew that she was beautiful.*
> *Jealous lover,*
> *Soon I shall make sweeter vows.*

Is friendship sufficient to her heart?
When one repeats, night and day:
Love for her!
Love!

Love for her!
Is a charming cry, worthy of her,
It comes from the heart.
Far from her enchanting gaze,
I wait, I seek, I call to her,
And I repeat, night and day:
Love for her! Love![16]

She re-reads that the tender confession, which Oscar has written down but did not dare to pronounce, a thousand times over. Radiant with joy, she appears before Elzine, who says to her: "You're bringing me good news."

"Alas, no," Thelemy replies, blushing. "Know the cause of the contentment that you were able to read immediately upon my face: every time I arrived in the palace, where I spent the happiest days of my life, I cannot resist an emotion to which everything gives rise. These places recall so many sweet memories! Everything here pleases me, I love everything here...even the air that one breathes here."

"Go on, Thelemy, seeing and hearing you, I experience a particular pleasure! But tell me...in the midst of

---

[16] As with most of the other verses that the author improvises, this one has a rhyme-scheme, but I have not attempted to reproduce it, because it cannot be done without too much injury to the meaning of the words—which is, in this instance, of paramount importance.

all these objects that flatter your eyes here, awaking your memories and interesting your heart, do you not sense any desire that attracts you and leads you to me?"

"I'm Athalise's daughter."

"Athalise's daughter!" Elzine replies, sadly.

"You're my mother's friend. That title is very dear to me, it inspires respect for you, and keen gratitude…"

"And nothing more?"

"The rest is for my mother."

"For your mother, Thelemy! And for me?"

"I don't have…I can't have the same love for you."

"Stop, Thelemy—you're breaking my heart."

"Forgive me, Madame…"

"Dear child!" Elzine went on, in an emotional voice. "So you love Athalise very much?"

"Who would not love a mother? A mother gives us life, opens our infancy, protects our first steps, dries our first tears, glories in our happiness. Her love follows us everywhere. She never abandons us…what's the matter, Madame? I see that you're growing pale and weeping."

"Continue, Thelemy—speak, speak again, go on speaking. I cannot weary of the sight of you, your speech, your sentiments. I love you too…perhaps I love you much more than I can tell you. So, then, Athalise?"

"Her condition still alarms my affection."

"May Heaven spare us such a misfortune—but in the end, if you lost her…"

"Oh, don't give me that cruel dread."

"What if she went away?"

"Her! Go away from me! Impossible. She would not want to. I would follow her anywhere. A mother never leaves her child."

"Cruel Thelemy," said Elzine, dissolving in tears. "No, you don't know, perhaps you'll never know, the harm you're doing to my heart. Listen. Sometimes, a mother is forced to leave her child. A misfortune, a terrible misfortune, powerful reasons...what can I say? In life, there are terrible, inexplicable situations of which you know nothing, as yet. A mother seems to abandon the child of her love. She swallows her tears, hides her sighs, and often...the victim of a rigorous duty, there where her cherished daughter lives, in the same place...close to her, in her arms...although all her senses are stirred, her soul excited, her heart broken by grief suffered in silence...even then, she cannot show...no one must see in her smile anything but a feigned indifference, anything in her eyes but a hidden sadness, anything in her face but a cold insensibility. Dear Thelemy, mourn for a mother forced to leave her child; pity her, weep for her. She is surely guilty, but she is even more unhappy. She languishes, she suffers; her heart might betray her; she is dead to life. Oh, my daughter..."

"You're upset, Madame. I don't know why, but I can see by your tears that you have much to lament."

"Of yes, much to lament—but at present, your voice consoles me."

"It will always console you."

"Always!"

"At least, I hope so. If you wanted to, you could take my mother's place, and be my mother too."

"Oh! What do you mean? Speak!"

"I love Oscar."

"I know that. Friendship binds you together."

"Friendship! No, it's much more now. Like me, Oscar also loves me, and it's..."

"Go on."

"Love."

"Wretched girl!"

105

"Great God, Madame, your expression makes me tremble. Listen to me—I haven't done anything wrong. It's Oscar who wants it. I haven't seduced him—but, seduced like him, I love him! Oh, I love him as much as my heart can love. My desires are pure, and if I could be his friend, his lover, his wife…"

"You! Oscar's wife! Impossible!"

"Alas, I know that. Oscar is a powerful prince. His mother reigns in a palace; mine lives on her charity. Me, I'm nothing…very little…I'm Athalise's daughter."

"Go away, Thelemy. I need to be alone. Let this secret remain between us. Renounce your love. Don't love Oscar any longer. I forbid you to. Don't come to the palace again. One day, I'll tell you…you'll know everything. Don't distress yourself. Embrace your friend. Go on, leave—return to Athalise's house, I tell you…but no, I'll come to see you, to console you. Goodbye! Goodbye…!"

Poor mother! Her sobs cut short her speech. She hugs Thelemy, makes a gesture bidding her to leave, and hides her tear-flooded face in her hands, repeating in a heart-rending voice: "How unhappy I am! My God! My God, have pity on me…!"

Confused and nonplussed, Thelemy goes away, weeping.

Already, though, Oscar has returned. He arrives, animated by the sweetest hope, and the first object that is offered to his eyes in the garden through which he is moving rapidly is the desolate Thelemy.

"Stop," he says. "Why these tears? They increase at my approach. You're not answering me, Thelemy— hurry up and speak, speak…explain yourself. I demand it, I command it…I beg you…"

"Oscar, we cannot see one another again. This is the last time."

"What a thing to say!"

"You mother…"

"Well?"

"Has forbidden me to love you. Our union is impossible. There is too great a distance between us."

"Dispel your fears; trust yourself to my faith. I shall see, speak to and convince my mother. She will be unable to resist my stern insistence. She will hear the voice of a son she loves, the prayer of a lover who adores you. She will unite us, I dare to assure you. Look, can you see her through the window of her apartment? Tender mother! She's following us with her eyes. She's looking at us with love; she's weeping. She's recognized me; she's calling me. Can you hear? Come on, Thelemy, let's run to throw ourselves at her feet."

So saying, he dragged Thelemy away. She made vain efforts to oppose him, but he heard nothing more. He had but one desire, one hope, one idea.

He fell at Elzine's feet, and presented Thelemy to her. "Mother," he said, "here is the friend of my childhood, the companion of my life, the wife that my heart has chosen. Consent to our happiness."

"Oscar, my darling son! Give up this madness!"

"Allow us to marry."

"Marry—you! What are you asking? Never! Never!"

"Well then, dread my despair. One more refusal, and I shall expire before your eyes."

"Stop, Oscar, I implore you! I'm trembling. You're forcing my hand. Know, then what the invincible obstacle is that is opposed to your desire: Thelemy is your sister." HUH ?!

107

"I'm Oscar's sister"

"Who, me? Thelemy's brother!"

"Yes, I'm your mother—both of you. My children! I've said it! I had to, to prevent a frightful crime. The terrible secret is out. Guard it well. My life, my honor and yours, everything depends on your silence. Athalise, that generous friend who has taken care of Thelemy...but nearby.... A noise...O Heaven! It's my husband! All is lost."

"Guards!" the governor cries. "Get rid of this young woman. You, Harold, take my son to his apartment. I confide him to your zeal. You'll answer to me for him with your head."

"Guards!" Oscar says. "Don't touch her—or fear my wrath!"

Elzine is carried to her bed, dying.

Adalbert has gone. Informed of his son's arrival, he was coming to see him when, as he approached Elzine's apartment, the discussion he overheard stopped him in his tracks. Struck by surprise on hearing it, he redoubled is attention. It was thus that chance disclosed a secret that a necessary prudence had rendered impenetrable for so many years.

What will the governor do now? The pride of rank, his betrayed trust, the mystery so long protected—everything irritates his troubled mind, and stifles the generous instincts in his soul. He can do anything, but already his sole desire is to abuse his authority. Retiring to his study, he thinks of nothing but plans of vengeance. He gives the strictest orders and refuses to yield to the pleas of Elzine, who wants to see him, to speak to him before dying.

Oscar learns of his mother's danger; a faithful friend has given him the sad news. His father has ordered him to remain in his apartment in vain. He seizes the sword of the guard who tries to retain him and threatens to strike anyone imprudent enough to dare to oppose his passage. The young prince, animated by anger and filial love, is allowed free passage; no one stops him. He runs to Elzine's apartment and open the door.

What a scene! Women in tears, a dismal silence, and his mother dying!

Elzine offers him her hand and points heavenwards. "Dear Oscar," she says, in a faint voice, "We shall see one another again in another world. It's the end; I'm going to die. Your father didn't want to hear my justification with my last sigh. You shall plead my cause with him. Oh, my son, come here, I can feel you still squeezing my icy hand. Receive my last embrace. Watch over the fate of Athalise and Thelemy... Farewell, Oscar, my dear Oscar! Remember your mother..."

Her eyes close and her voice expires on her lips while pronouncing Thelemy's name.

Oscar's despair is impossible to describe. The loss of a mother is one of those misfortunes that, absorbing all the strength of grief, leaves nothing for its expression. Oscar sometimes busts into jerky sobs, and sometimes, motionless next to the inanimate Elzine, his fixed stare considers her with that frightful calm, that stupor, which is the sign of a profound depression.

Finally, his sensibility awakes; he is drawn away from the apparatus of death that surrounds him. Furiously, he cuts through the tumultuous waves of people assembled in front of the palace, and shouts loud demands for someone to save his benefactress. Elzine is dead to them, but she still lives on in the unhappiness that he has consoled.

Oscar arrives at Athalise's house; he finds no more than debris. Frightened by what he sees, he cannot believe his eyes. He asks questions. He learns that an order by the governor, published several days before, has caused the house to be demolished, that Athalise and Thelemy have been banished forever from Moravia, and that no one was able to help them without incurring the prince's ill-favor.

Crushed, deaf to all that he hears, he no longer knows what will become of him, which way to turn. He advances at hazard along any road that offers itself to him. He questions everyone he meets in his passage, and hastens to pursue his search in order to save his mother's friend and his beloved sister, if there is still time.

4

Meanwhile, having been thrown out of their home, Athalise and Thelemy are fleeing before the guards who are pursuing them. Wandering, abandoned by Heaven and human beings alike, without shelter, without friends, they drag themselves along the road of exile, whose extent makes their hearts quail in advance.

Athalise, barely recovered from a painful illness, feels her strength ebbing away with every passing moment. Her soul alone still sustains her, showing itself superior to adversity. She has doomed herself for her friend. That idea gives her the courage to bear her suffering. The misfortune that degrades and humiliates timid characters revives the energy of nobler souls.

Thelemy, however, in despair at the prospect of so much misery, follows her adoptive mother in a flood of tears. "O God," she said, "the whole world has abandoned us. Look, all eyes turn away from us! People avoid us. Oscar too. Does he not know that I'm suffering?"

"You must forget him," Athalise replies.

"Forget him! When love is devouring me!"

"He's your brother, Thelemy."

"He only became so in my eyes a few days ago, and he was my friend, my lover since I first drew breath. Can the heart forget such a long happiness for a single moment of ill luck?"

"You're raving, my child—don't aggravate the torments of our situation. It's frightful, as you can see."

"O Heaven! Have you given me birth only for misfortune?"

"Calm down, I implore you," said Athalise, compassionately.

"Oh, it's only for you that I'm weeping."

"Dear child!"

"You have done everything for Thelemy."

"Be quiet! Silence, Thelemy!"

"I owe you everything. I owe you more than life, and it's me—me!—who will be the death of you!"

"Shut up! You're hurting me."

"You've never abandoned me! You weren't my mother, though, and the woman who was…"

"What are you saying? What complaint dare you make? Dear child, pain is causing your heart to sin. Don't blame your mother. You have only your own misfortune; she has two of them. One alone—yours—is the most horrible of all for her. Your mother cannot resist that. I know her. Perhaps, even at this very moment, on the brink of losing her life, she is blessing the child that is condemning her."

Thelemy utters a dolorous cry. "Mother! Forgive me, Mother! Forgive your wretched child. Kneel down, Athalise—let's pray for her!"

If a pure soul, a fervent prayer and religious tears please the God by whose command everything lives and everything suffers, the pleas of Athalise and Thelemy will reach him.

Two days pass thus. Already need is making itself felt.

"Let's stop," says Athalise. "I can't go on any longer. I'm cold, I'm thirsty…a little water!" And, as she pronounces these swords of distress, she collapses at the foot of a tree.

Thelemy realizes her friend's danger. Her exhausted body is reanimated. Her only thought is the desire to save her. She runs, searching everywhere for urgent assistance…perhaps the last. She would give her life to find a limpid stream, a spring, her only hope, her only refuge.

She advances into the fields, through brambles and stony gravel. Her delicate feet are bruised, but she feels no pain.

She covers a great deal of ground like that, but all her efforts are in vain. Finally, at the corner of a wood, beneath a solitary rock, she believes that she hears the gentle murmur of a cascade springing forth. She flies in that direction.

Clear water is sprinkling the greenery. She fills her two hands with it, and, breathlessly, covered with cold sweat, she hurries back to Athalise….

Great God! She is lying on the ground. Her head is tilted in the direction in which she saw Thelemy depart. Her lips are parted and seem to be repeating a final farewell. Thelemy thinks that she is unconscious.

She calls out. No reply.

"Athalise!" she says. "Wake up, dear friend, it's Thelemy! She's bring you life. Athalise! Can you hear me?"

All is silent. Thelemy is gripped by fear; the water escapes her hands. She takes Athalise in her arms, hugs her to her distraught bosom, inundates her with tears, and repeats her name in the most dolorous tone imaginable.

Oh, how heart-rending is the voice of Thelemy then! But vain efforts, alas! No more hope! Athalise will never see her again. Her breast is cold; her heart no longer beats beneath the hand of her desolate daughter; her eyes have closed forever.

Thelemy no longer has the strength to resist this final misfortune. She runs wildly along the road. A carriage goes by. She throws herself in front of the horses. The carriage stops. A stranger gets out. Thelemy does not speak, but her hand points to the object of her cruel distress. She drags the stranger, who studies Athalise attentively. Thelemy's eyes are fixed on the gaze of the protector that Heaven has sent her.

It does not take him long to perceive that all medical aid is futile. He pronounces death. Suddenly, Thelemy's colorless lips display a frightful smile. Her head swims. She babbles word that are the frightful indication of the onset of madness.

At that moment, Oscar, who has been following Thelemy's trail for a long time, perceives her from afar. He races toward her, shouting: "Thelemy! Thelemy! I've finally found you... O Heaven! What a state you're in! It's me, look—do you recognize me?"

Thelemy looks at him but no longer recognizes him. Oscar takes her in his arms; she loses consciousness there. While the stranger carries Athalise's body, the despairing young prince supports Thelemy. They climb into the carriage, and it draws away.

5

The stranger was Odolzi, a famous physician who devoted his universally-admired talents to the sufferings of humankind. In a château set in the foothills of a mountain chain, shaded by trees—an enchanting location favorable to the secrets of his art—he gave to poor wretches, whom unexpected disasters, various misfortunes and lost reason had exiled from the world, the most expert care, the precious fruit of profound study. In that dwelling, embellished on all sides by cheerful nature, dwelt insane individuals who had once been happy and envied; objects of pity now, though still full of life, they did not know that they had lived for a society by which they had been permanently forgotten.

A dolorous depiction of human destiny!

Alas, more than one woman, victim of an excessively heightened sensitivity, unjustly betrayed, still demanded from the mute echo of solitude the lost love of a lover still adored.

There it was that Thelemy was taken.

Oscar was inconsolable. He no longer wanted to leave Thelemy. He looked after her, followed her everywhere. More than once he whispered the sweet names of brother and sister in her ear, but Thelemy was insensible to everything he said. Nothing could extract her from her silent distress.

Several days passed, and Oscar's despair testified that he had lost all hope. Odolzi tried to bring some relief to his pain. "Come, prince," he said to him one day,

Come and witness an interesting scene, which might perhaps momentarily restore the reason of the friend for whom you weep. There are few souls sufficiently lost to nature to be insensible to the effects of harmonious music. Various successful trials have already made me proud of a discovery by means of which a few days of genius may obtain surprising results. The future will complete what I have begun.

"In the frightful abandonment by others and themselves that the unfortunates to which I devote my cares are often found, dementia does not absorb all the faculties. The intelligence is dead, the reason absent, the mind asleep, but the soul is awake. There is a heart that lights up again at the first spark of a new sensation. Sentiment has a memory that is not lost. Love is the romance of life, and neither feels nor reasons in the passions of woman.

"Music, especially, exerts its active influence on tender souls. Who among is, in advancing through life, has not come across a song heard in a time already distant from us, but which recalls affections dear to our memory? The harmonious sound of a harp, the brisk sound of a guitar, a ballad sung in happier times by a woman we have loved. all these sensations reproduce themselves with a charm that penetrates us, seduces us, moves us. That is why melancholy songs soothe pain. Their softness restores calm to a heart tormented by a well-being irredeemably lost. You shall judge for yourself."

Immediately, a signal having been given, a shepherd appears on top of the mountain. An invisible music becomes audible. It is so delightful, so plaintive, that Oscar is moved by it, in spite of his somber sadness. The valley from which these delightful chords are coming seems to him to be a magical place.

Soon, Thelemy arrives. She climbs up the rock and, having reached the summit, sits down. Her crooked elbow is set on the rock and her abandoned head inclines toward the supportive arm. The shepherd begins to sing.

Let laughter fade!
Fair Elmire bade,
Her shepherd swain.
You dare complain
Whene'er I sigh,
And bid me try
Love none but thee.
All around me
Declares, betrayed:
Let laughter fade!

Within the vales
The echo hails:
Let laughter fade!

The wave so pure
Cannot endure.
All form decays.
Cold winter slays,
The green leaf browns,
The wind discrowns
The woodland flower.
You see its power
Declares, betrayed:
Let laughter fade!

Within the vales,
The echo hails:
Let laughter fade!

My love, delight,
Look on, shine bright,
All once was charm,
His smile was warm.
There is no truth,
In dreams of youth.
Farewell, I say,
My flight away'
Declares, betrayed:
Let laughter fade!

Within the vales
The echo hails:
Let laughter fade!

"See!" says Odolzi. "Thelemy is getting up, asking for a harp. Let's move closer—but don't show yourself yet, and above all, don't interrupt. Let her give in to all that the music has just caused her to experience. Soon, perhaps, she might recognize you."

Transported by this hope, Oscar is obedient to Odolzi's advice. He hides behind her. Oh, how Thelemy's divine figure is outlined at the top of the mountain! What grace her touching melancholy gives her, with the pallor of her face, and her hair floating in the magical hand that causes the strings of the harp to quiver as they resonates in the wind!

Oscar admires her; he thinks he is looking at a celestial being, an angel inspired by Heaven.

"My dear Thelemy," says the physician, "what sentiment are you experiencing at this moment?"

"An illness that pleases me. My heart is on fire...my ideas are confused; but once I was very...exceedingly close to him. He loved me then! Now...I'm very unhappy!"

"Thelemy!" Oscar exclaims.

"Silence!" Odolzi says to him.

"Oh my God!" Thelemy continues. "I thought I heard...but no. I was mistaken. No more happiness for me! So I want to die, but I can't!"

"Do you want to weep forever, then?"

"To weep forever," she says.

"Calm yourself. Everyone here loves you."

"No, he doesn't love me anymore. He mustn't love me anymore."

"Why do you fear that?"

"Why, he asks! It's obvious that he doesn't know everything. Well, I'll tell you. Listen:

I still live on! Just now I said:
Weep forever, and never die!
Heaven wants me to live instead,
Farewell to joy, fine days goodbye.
They are no more, my tears I shed
For Oscar, and our love run dry.
I live on! And just now I said:
I'll weep forever, and never die!

I loved him so, my love's not fled!
But he was set to let me lie.
The ingrate thinks that I'm misled,
But I know him—I want to die.
I weep while wishing I were dead

118

For Oscar and our love run dry.
I still live on! Just now I said:
I'll weep forever, and never die!

I long to see him, hear his tread
But he'll no longer heed my cry.
My name was once his wine and bread
But now he wants to let me lie.
I'll always weep, despite my dread
For Oscar and our love run dry.
I still live on! Just now I said:
I'll weep forever, and never die!

How he loved me! "Until I'm dead,"
He said to me, "I'll ne'er deny
I'll always love your pretty head."
But then it was I had to cry
I'm crying still, more tears I'll shed
For Oscar and our love run dry.
I still live on! Just now I said:
I'll weep forever, and never die!

I was lovely, and he well-bred,
Our friendship easy to espy;
By equal example we were led,
No one doubted the reason why.
But you can see the tears I shed
For Oscar and our love run dry.
I still live on! Just now I said:
I'll weep forever, and never die!

Suddenly, all the good times fled
My mother told the reason why
He and I could never be wed.

Alone beneath the hostile sky,
Forgive me for the tears I shed
For Oscar and our love run dry.
I still live on! Just now I said:
I'll weep forever, and never die!

Devoid of kin, of blood dry-bled,
No brother's voice to say: "Don't cry."
No heart to call my heart inbred.
Unhappiness causes smiles to fly.
Alas, I dread the tears I shed
For Oscar and our love run dry.
I still live on! Just now I said:
I'll weep forever, and never die!

All life on earth moves on ahead
Let unkind fate my birth belie
Orphan me in my mother's bed
And o'er her tomb force me to sigh;
I'll not forswear the tears I shed
For Oscar and our love run dry.
I still live on! Just now I said:
I'll weep forever, and never die!

And thus it is, my fortune read,
Devoid of any human tie.
The love he owed me all has sped,
Wretched am I, the end is nigh,
And that is why my tears I shed
For Oscar and our love run dry.
I still live on! Just now I said:
I'll weep forever, and never die!

Thelemy's song has come to an end. Oscar reveals himself to her sight. He covers her hand with kisses and tears. "Dear Thelemy," he cries, "will you never recognize your brother?"

"You, my brother? Oh, if it were only true. But what are you saying, wretch? A brother, me? I have none. I have never had one." Then, in a whisper, she added: "Silence! Guard that terrible secret well. If anyone heard us, all would be lost. For the sake of my mother's honor, no one must know that I'm her daughter. Do you know it yourself?

I'm the child of her loving lie.
I still live on! Just now I said:
I'll weep forever, and never die!"

"Dear friend! My sister! You whom I love, whom I shall love forever, you recognized the voice of Oscar, then."

"Oscar! You? Oscar! Yes, it's him!"

After that cry, which echoes distantly in the valley, Thelemy runs away in terror, and the edge of the wood soon hides her from every gaze.

"Don't follow her, prince," says Odolzi. "Avoid the danger of prolonged overexcitement. She's too weak to sustain so many sensations are the same time. I'll send someone to find her; they'll bring her back to the château. Trust in my zeal, and be reassured."

Darkness fell. An hour earlier, various messages from the court had arrived. Prince Adalbert had discovered his son's retreat, and Harold had orders to bring him back, with Odolzi. Everyone was prepared to obey the governor.

Meanwhile, the search for Thelemy is in vain. She has not been found. She has not returned to the château. A horn is blown on the mountain. That signal brings everyone together. The search is resumed in the valley, in the forest and everywhere else. Thelemy does not appear. She does not reply to the voices that call her. There is no indication of the refuge she has chosen.

The night is exceedingly dark. Torches are shining everywhere. Guided by their distant light, they finally arrive at the bank of a torrent, and the first light of day revealed a clue that chilled all their frightened hearts. A veil floating above the waters of the torrent is hanging from a wild willow tree. It is the veil that Thelemy was wearing. This news is hurriedly conveyed to the château.

Odolzi orders silence to be maintained regarding a suspicion that time alone can clarify, and, in accordance with his advice, they take advantage of a profound slumber into which the prince had been plunged, by the fatigue of all the torments he has suffered, to transport him while still asleep.

The signal for departure is given. As rapid as the wind, the governor's chargers follow the road to Olmutz.

The Pursuit of Lord Ruthwen
(continued)

VI

Aubrey stopped speaking. His two friends had shed tears frequently during the story of the young Moravian woman's misfortunes. Nadoor Ali loved Oscar's character, sentiments and conduct, but Léonti had only been struck by the fate of Thelemy. He was still lending an attentive ear and seemed to be awaiting the end of an interrupted story. Aubrey remained silent.

"My friend," Léonti said to him then, "why stop at the moment of your story that is the most interesting to me? Tell us what became of Thelemy. All her links of existence and affection were broken. She was only bound to the world by misfortune. Betrayed in her hopes and detesting life, she ought to have died. But if it is true that the torrent had put an end to her troubles, what resemblance can she bear to the cruel man we are pursuing? You promised that, and that's what I want to know.

"A female vampire lover! My mind rejects an impossible horror. My friend, a woman is an enchanting creature. Ornamented with all the graces and beautified by all the generous sentiments, she is nature's masterpiece. Seductive by virtue of her beauty, more sympathetic by virtue of her weakness, always a victim, she yields to oppression and never oppressed. Forgetting the happiness she gives, she remembers only that which she receives, and her heart, which is so tender, replete with

potential for loving, suffering and forgiving, has no im-
pulse at all toward hatred, even less toward vengeance."

Aubrey resumed his story:

The Story of the Young Moravian Woman
(continued)

6

On returning to his father's palace, Oscar went over the story of Thelemy's flight into the forest a thousand times: the cruel night that had hidden her from all the searches; and, finally, the veil found at daybreak, still damp with the waters of the torrent. He did not doubt that those pitiless waters had swallowed the person who was for him both the most adored lover and the most cherished sister.

All the brilliant fêtes of the court, the splendor of a superlative rank and the perils surrounding glory could not distract him from his regret.

Time bears away all transient pleasures, but a profound anguish lives in memory, and, even in fleeing, it leaves a painful impression in the depths of the soul that is never effaced.

Several years went by. Oscar was still insensible to the desires of a thousand beauties desperate to please him—but the ever-increasing ambitions of power and the pride of a famous name made the governor of Moravia determined to choose a wife for his son. It was necessary to obey.

Already, everything is in preparation for the celebration of a royal wedding. The nuptial headband adorns the forehead of Princess Amélie. She is about to plight her troth. The altar is dressed. The hymn commences. Oscar pronounces the hymeneal vows...

Suddenly, the church door pens. A harp resonates. A voice sings:

> I still live on! Just now I said:
> I'll weep forever, and never die!"

And they see...

coinciding w/ each other, nice

The Pursuit of Lord Ruthwen
(continued)

VII

"O Heaven!" Léonti cries.

"What's the matter?"

"It's her!"

"Who?"

"Bettina!"

"Yes," says Bettina, "it's me. It was me that you saw in Naples and heard in Rome, who had reappeared to your sight to tell you that the perfidious stranger is here, all-powerful in the court of Modena."

"Our enemy is in Modena?" says Aubrey.

"He is the prime minister, and calls himself Lord Seymour."

"Lord Seymour? Is that really his name?"

"It's the vampire, I tell you—I recognized him."

"Let's hasten to take our revenge."

"Stop!" Bettina adds. "The enterprise is difficult, let's undertake it with prudence. The moment has not yet come to carry our vengeance to its climax. The governor of the palace is the faithful friend of the prince, the Duke of Modena. He hates the insolent minister who is betraying his master's confidence. He has been forewarned of the important secret that I have just revealed, and I'm awaiting his orders."

"Dear Bettina," says Léonti, moved to tears, "is it really you that I see again? If this is not a dream, if you have returned to me, don't seek to flee once again from an unhappy man who loves you—remain with your lover."

"A religious vow forbids me that until the day of the vampire's death."

"But for mercy's sake, take pity my plight—explain to us the inconceivable mystery of your return. Tell us how, in what place and by what supernatural power you came back to live?"

In response, Bettina smiles and promises to tell that incredible story. She invites Nadoor Ali and Aubrey to sit down beside her, looks at Léonti lovingly, and begins in these terms:

"When, in haste to follow perfidious advice, and filled with the desire to persuade my father, you left me with the stranger, both of us, alas, being young and innocent, we did not know that crime often borrows the language of virtue, and that treason hides beneath the mild exterior of friendship.

"That odious stranger was the vampire announced by the prophecies of Elmoda. Having become his victim, I fell down dying on the sandy shore; but the desire to see you once more before leaving you forever reanimated my failing strength, and I dragged myself as far as the place where I heard the sound of your beloved voice. I saw you, my dear lover, and, less unhappy, my extinguished gaze was able to bid you a final farewell.

"Do you still remember that dolorous farewell…?

"But what was I saying? Whether animated by the rapid breath of divine inspiration, or by the burning of a love stronger than life, my heart outlived its faculties. Then, O Léonti, as I expired before your eyes, I did not believe that I was dying forever, and it seemed to me that my soul, as it escaped me, gave me the soothing reassurance that I would see you again.

"The lily and the white rose do not flourish in funereal fields. Their culture, beloved of Heaven, is only pleased to embellish the happy refuge of hope—and yet, their verdant stems were already beginning to rise up over my tomb, covered with a mother's tears and a lover's kisses, when, by means of a prodigy superior to the human mind, everything seemed to stir around me.

"I felt a fire in my veins that devoured me. My eyes shone in the profound gloom, my burning lips quivered, the quaking earth opened up, and like terrifying claps of thunder, these terrible words resounded in mid-air: 'Vampire woman! Emerge from the tomb!'

"I appeared then to a new life. At first, darting distressed glances around me, I saw nothing but dark scenes. I was alone, separated from other living beings, whom my presence chilled with fear. The moon, friend of our climes, was in its decline, and lit with its uncertain clarity a distant horizon that fled from my sight. The imposing calm of the night added to my mental confusion.

"I did not know what to do. My disordered thoughts only allowed me to comprehend a vague desire for vengeance. But on whom could I slake the blind fury that was making my blood boil? Who was the guilty party that I ought to punish, the enemy that I had to strike down?

"Forgive me, Léonti! I don't know what cruel divinity had upset all my senses, but of all the objects that I had known in my first life, I only remembered you, and this heart that had loved you so much—can you believe it?—this heart formed the barbaric project of driving you to despair. Yes, it was you, it was you that I wanted to pursue, and that is why, a docile plaything of an imperious, inexplicable, horrible destiny, Bettina chose for a victim the lover that she still adored.

"That frightful idea tormented my soul, however, and as soon as I had expelled all bitterness therefrom, a softer emotion calmed my bewildered senses, my tears flowed, my cries resounded, and my errant footsteps steered at hazard. There was a gondola close to the shore. I fell into it and, floating in the open sea, I abandoned myself to the divine influence that was guiding my involuntary movements.

"Dawn was breaking, coloring the surrounding mountains with its first fires. Everything came to life in the lovely valleys and the green hills. The morning laborers confided their hopes to the fertile ground. A pure and melodious song rose into the sky. Young women grouped on a river-bank shaded by trees replied to hymns repeated on the opposite bank. That sweet harmony, which rendered the majestic spectacle of the waters even more delightful, brought a delicious calm into my soul.

"In that intoxicating ecstasy, the first need I experienced was to offer my prayers to the author of nature. I was penetrated by that pious duty when a wood came in sight. I guided my boat to the shore and raced in the direction of a chapel consecrated to seafarers. My knees bent on the steps of a revered altar of a God whom misfortune never implores in vain—but at the very moment when my prayers were rising up to Heaven, I felt my eyelids becoming heavy, and involuntarily, a sudden drowsiness overtook my senses. It was then that a soothing dream gave me a glimpse of a happier destiny.

"A celestial angel appeared to me. I saw him. He was suspended in mid-air, an azure cloud sustaining his deployed wings, and his dazzling aureole announced the messenger of a powerful God. 'Young woman of the Lido,' he said, 'prayer has moved the Eternal. By virtue of a favor that can only emanate from divine grandeur, your soul, pure in its early days, will conserve its bounty in the new life that will open up before you. You shall not be the terror of mortals, like those monsters, the detested scourge of haven and humankind.

vampire from God

"'Woman, often misunderstood, always oppressed on the Earth of vain errors, proud of fulfilling a mission worthy of her, should only return here to be the terror of the guilty and the safeguard of virtuous lives. That is the will of the God you adore. Bettina, you will be destined henceforth to protect the object of our chaste love. Awaken and go forth; direct your steps eastward. Heaven will guide you, but you shall not be reunited forever with the lover you shall find again until the vampire whose victim you were is rendered to the earth of tombs, which will soon close upon him for all eternity. Promise to obey the celestial will.'

"'I swear!' I cried...and with those words, I woke up. My opened eyes searched the sky in vain for the images that sleep had presented to me. Palpitating and inspired, I left for the sea-shore. A boatman came in response to my voice. I ordered him to take me away. I don't know whether what I had just seen had imprinted a divine expression on all my features, but the dweller of the sea-shore looked at me in astonishment, and his boat, docile to the oar, immediately, fled over the water.

"During that journey, of whose duration I was unconscious, the boatman accompanied me everywhere. He was my faithful guide in the cities through which I traveled, but when we arrived at the extremity of Italy, his zeal slackened. He interrogated me as to my further course. My mysterious replies gave birth to suspicions in his mind that rendered my situation more difficult with every passing moment. I did not know myself where I was going and I was relying on celestial inspiration to head me where my destiny intended. It was in the midst of such uncertainties that we reached the Neapolitan shore…"

At this point. Bettina's story is interrupted by a sound that makes her shiver. A messenger comes in and gives her an order from the court. Bettina reads it and says to the messenger: "I will come with you." Then, turning to Léonti, she says: "Until tomorrow; I'll expect you at the palace."

"At the palace?" says Aubrey.

"Yes," Bettina replies. "The Duc d'Albini, who is the governor, will furnish us with the means to confound our enemy."

"Stay here, Bettina!" says Léonti.

"I can't."

"Stop!"

"Farewell!"

And then, as light as a shadow, she flees from the three friends, astonished that they can no longer see her, and even more astonished to have seen her at all.

Bettina's arrival and discourse had produced such an impression on Nadoor Ali that, more than once, while she spoke, his extreme astonishment became manifest. As soon as she has gone, he says: "I can't understand the mysterious crimes of the enemy you're pursuing, and yet, they remind me of a perfidious friend that I am led to believe to be the author of my cruelest misfortunes."

"And to what nation did the author of your misfortunes belong?" Aubrey asks. "Was he from your homeland?"

"No, he was English."

"English? What was his name?"

"I don't know."

"Nor do I," Aubrey continues, "but a presentiment suggests to me that we have to avenge ourselves on a common enemy. Let us join forces to crush him. Tomorrow we shall go to the palace. While waiting for daylight, let's take advantage of the time remaining to us. Tell, us, my dear Nadoor Ali, the cause of the dark distress that is devouring you. I remember that in Rome, sitting on the sandy bank of the Tiber, on the brink of gathering in the outpourings of a heart, we were already listening to you—and your voice pronounced the name of Cymodora."

That name made Nadoor Ali shiver again. His face went pale, his eyes flashed and he manifested a sharp agitation in all his senses that he struggled in vain to control. He stood up and opened a window that overlooked the fields of Modena. Dusk was beginning to cover the green of the surrounding countryside with its veils, but the sky was starry. Everything was calm, except for a fresh breeze agitating the treetops, and, like a string breaking on an idle harp, the occasional harsh cry of a nocturnal bird.

Nadoor Ali stared at the landscape unfurled before him, and remained motionless in that state for some time. Finally, he emerged from his profound meditation, drew nearer to Aubrey and Léonti—who, observing his emotion, had not dared to distract him—and said to them: "Friends, as you wish it, I shall confide to you my most dangerous secrets."

Then he put his hand to his brow, reflected momentarily, and began to tell the story of his life:

The Story of Nadoor Ali and Cymodora

1

To obey and tremble is the destiny of the peoples of our climes. Made illustrious by military glory, does a warrior enjoy shining favor? The foremost slave of a proud court, a single instant suffices to annihilate his numerous services. His suspect faith becomes criminal. Torture is near to triumph. The same voice that raises up a favorite to the steps of the throne remorselessly orders the horrible fall of a minister who ceases to please; a prompt, inevitable, terrible death is the perennial law of a pitiless master, and the price of a rapid elevation to grandeur.

Such was my father's fate. He was too powerful; he seemed culpable. A cruel command raised the guards of his own palace against him. He was slain, and such is the brutalization of soldiers of despotism that his companions in arms, whom he had so often led to victory and upon whom he had heaped rewards, did not hesitate to plunge a dagger into the generous heart of the leader who had protected them for so long.

At the time of that bloody catastrophe, which deprived me of an adored father and my entire family, I was in the army. Already proud to be testing my young courage, I was fighting in the valley of Firan.[17] A devoted slave, escaping the carnage at the palace, ran to bring me the terrible news. Outraged by my father's disgrace, in the first surge of my despair I wanted to precipitate myself through the tide of warriors and at least perish at the hands of an enemy, but the faithful Azem, retrieving me from that impetuous ardor, guided my charger far from the places where my life was simultaneously threatened by the blades of battle and the will of the prince who had condemned lives consecrated to his defense.

Forced to abandon my homeland, I wandered for some time as a fugitive, devoured by my misery and detesting life—but, having been born of a father who lad left to future generations a name redoubtable in war, an insatiable lust for glory reanimated my depressed spirits. I directed my steps to the banks of the Ganges.

The Marathas[18] had invaded the territory of the Rajah of Benares. The greatest disorder reigned universally among a people more accustomed to the peace of seraglios than the fierce clash of arms. Boats were trembling under the burden of heaped-up riches, and the frightened Indians were fleeing in haste with a precious burden that called upon them a danger that they wanted to avoid.

---

[17] Firan (Bérard uses the alternative spelling of Pharan) is in the southern Sinai desert; the valley contains an important oasis.

[18] The Marathas (*Marattes* in French) extended an empire by means of the gradual conquest of much of the Indian subcontinent between 1674 and 1818, when it was overthrown by the British. This reference is inconsistent with the date that subsequently sets the story in the early 1600s.

I entered Benares in the midst of the tumult. Impatient to risk new perils, my blood was boiling in my veins and seemed about to cause my heart to burst. I advanced toward the palace; it as deserted and already pressed by the approach of the enemy. Surrounded by guards who threatened to become disobedient to his orders, the Rajah was considering flight himself. Then I appeared.

"Prince!" I cried. "In the midst of the misfortunes that surround you and your unworthy soldiers, trembling before your enemies, permit a stranger to offer the assistance of his virile courage. Flight is the shameful refuge of the weak. Guards! Will you suffer that I, raised far from these borders, and yet ready to fulfill a glorious duty that belongs to you, should fight alone for a master that you have sworn to defend? Let my voice arm you. The Marathas, frightened by a surprise attack, will flee before us, I dare to assure you. Victory will crown our intrepidity. All of you follow Nadoor Ali; he will march at your head. Let's go."

At these words, whether because my name succeeded in reanimating their confidence or because they were inspired by the warrior ardor that my face and words displayed with a sudden need to repel shame and prefer a glorious death, I saw them gather around me and swear to win a victory or to die. Immediately, I led them forth. We fell upon the enemy ranks. The most immediate success surpassed my hopes. The Marathas were dispersed, and I brought his guards back to the Rajah's feet, astonished to be returning as victors.

In the intoxication of unexpected good fortune, the prince did not know how to express his gratitude to me. I refused the riches that he offered me, but I accepted the command of his army, and from then on, attached to his court, I became his counselor and his friend.

A long peace soon returned to Benares the soft idleness that reigns in the palaces of Asia. Aloes perfumed the air. The bayaderes reappeared. Their voluptuous dances were combined with the harmony of concerts, and love of pleasure, resuming its empire, dispelled the very memory of the Marathas, a bellicose people tormented by the turbulent spirit of conquest.

It was during a brilliant fête that I saw the Rajah's daughter for the first time. Surrounded by a company of young slave-girls, who presented the attractions of all climes to the delighted eye, Azolida was more seductive still: lithe, charming and universally admired, one would have judged that her beauty would have called her to the highest rank of all if her birth had not distanced her therefrom. Never had the amorous harp quivered more charmingly than when her hand plucked its harmonious strings.

I had learned the arts of Europe, and sometimes, beside Azolida, my lyre gave voice to chords unknown to her. Then, after a gentle prelude, I would repeat this Arab song:

> Flower of the morning, I feel adoration for you
>   When I see you, love devours me
>   My heart and my senses reel,
>   And my eyes search for you again
>   Although I can no longer see you.
> Flower of the morning, I shall see you no more.
>
> Flower of the morning, sole charm of my life,
>   You will soon delight me,
>   Honor calls, I must obey,

And in the fields of Araby
Do battle, perhaps to die.
Flower of the morning, farewell, I must go.

Flower of the morning, know my aspiration,
In the battles to which I go,
If Heaven should spare my life
I have the hope on my return
In loving you to be lover forever.
Flower of the morning, I shall love you forever.
Forever![19]

Attentive and delighted, Azolida loved the expression of my voice, and she was still listening when the song had ended.

Meanwhile, renown brought us the admired name of a descendant of those cavalier kings who had once appeared not far from the deserts of Arabia. I wanted to see a people so famous for courage and elegant mores. I promised the Rajah to gather knowledge precious to our region regarding European arts of war and politics. He consented to the useful voyage, but stipulated that its duration should be limited, and when I left, Azolida's tears urged me to hasten my return.

2

I am reaching a period of my life when further misfortunes, perhaps more frightful than the first, inflicted a

---

[19] As this supposed song is allegedly translated from the Arabic, its French rhymes are presumably a superfluous artifice, so I have made no attempt to reproduce them in this literal translation.

cruel wound on my heat that has never healed. I had been in the beautiful countries to which my admiration for warrior peoples had led me for some while when an order from the Rajah recalled me of the court of Benares. I obeyed, but, yielding to a desire I had to travel through places rendered forever famous by heroic exploits, I initially headed for Athens. There I interrogated the sparse ruins, the illustrious land trodden by the charges of Attica, sprinkled with the blood of heroes whose graves, covered with wild moss, have disappeared from the sad view of those who seek their traces.

One day, lost in a reverie on the shore of the Aegean Sea, I was admiring the islands with which it is dotted, sitting beneath a solitary palm tree, I heard the rustle of a tunic. Like a nimble gazelle detached from the sprightly herds that inhabit the shady banks of the Euphrates, a young beauty hurtle forth, passing swiftly in front of me, and the sight of her left me a surprise and delight of which my expressions can only give an imperfect idea. She was tall, with a lofty head and a proud stride, her hair floating free. A bow and arrows were suspended from her shoulder. Her hand held a lyre, and she thus combined the various attributes of the fabulous goddesses of the Greeks.

My charmed eyes followed the daughter of Athens from a distance. I approached hr without being perceived and, hidden nearby, I listened to the wild chords that her bold fingers played on the shore.

"Impetuous winds, blow in the plain, raise waves on the sea. Fearlessly, I appear in the midst of ruins. I love the noise of tempests. My lyre resonates in the quivering of storms. I flee the air sullied by the presence of men. I am free."

Thus sang Cymodora. Her pride, her energy and the harshness of a language that seems only to belong to the courageous Greeks, the honor of heroic centuries, made a profound impression on me. Curious to know the fate of that extraordinary woman, I stood up and introduced myself to her gaze.

As soon as she saw me she seized an arrow, and her taut bow directed it at me. I ducked my head and asked her to listen to me. My supplicant attitude astonished and disarmed her. I advanced toward her—but then, resuming her swift course, she ran through the ruins, climbed the hill and disappeared.

No, I shall never be able to describe the delightful disturbance that was left in my soul by the charms, the voice and the absence of Cymodora. For a long time, I stared in the direction in which she had fled. I wandered along the shore. I looked for the soft sand that had conserved her footprints. I thought I could still see her there, running; I recognized a few traces of her passage, and my enchanted heart asked Cymodora once again she had come from.

Tormented by the pleasure of having seen her, and he dread of never seeing her again, I started to draw away. I walked at hazard, and an involuntary alarm drew me toward the place where she had panicked on seeing me. I was looking down at the ground. I perceived writing on a piece of paper covered with a few strands of wild ivy. I lifted them up and parted them, and found lines gathered from the Greek muse who sang of love and her unhappiness, and was seen to perish on a rock, famed for her last farewell.

I could not understand how Cymodora, who was irritated by the mere appearance of a man, had been able to read the delirious expression of the most tender sentiment without emotion. But new characters were traced after the immortal verses of Sappho! I was impatient to know the thoughts of the daughter of Athens; they were to remain forever graven in my memory. I read.

Cymodora's Pensées

Unhappy Sappho! What use was your genius? Phaon was an ingrate.[20] *All men are.*

Women! Shun love if you fear abandonment and unhappiness. It brings in its train the dolor that withers beauty, and the absence that leads to oblivion.

With what haste you flee to your doom, Palmyra![21] *A charming virgin who blushes on being admired, you follow an adored lover. He promises you happiness. You believe in an illusion that dazzles you, and, delirious and confused, you fly into his arms. Where are you going, imprudent woman? The intoxication of love only lasts as long as a dream. Oh, how painful the awakening will be! Soon you will be the image of a colorless flower. Your eyes will lose their gleam, your lips their vermilion freshness and your soft gaze, worthy of inspiring the*

---

[20] In Greek myth, Phaon was an ugly old boatman in Mytilene, on the island of Lesbos, who was given a rejuvenating ointment by Aphrodite after ferrying her across the sea. The amorous conquests he subsequently made were said by Ovid, Lucian and others to have included the poet Sappho, who allegedly killed herself when he moved on.
[21] Palmyra was a city in Syria, destroyed in 270 AD. Its destruction is the subject of a famous lyrical lament by Thomas Love Peacock, published in 1806, but Cymodora cannot possibly have been familiar with that work (although Bérard probably was) and must be quoting a much earlier source, seemingly out of context.

smile of the gods, will no longer obtain any but the success of despair: the pity of mortals. Cruelly, they will pass by without looking at you, and, while still young, you will learn that, for a discarded lover, life is nothing but a slow agony.

And you, daughter of the Orient! Bayaderes who shine on other shores; young odalisques, vain ornaments of Asian palaces, what is your fate? Slavery.

I, a daughter of the desert, hate men. I flee from them. I am free!

What reflections did I not make then upon that liberty, the sentiment of which is born with life, which leads so many generous hearts astray, and which no mortal possesses?

"I am free," Cymodora said. She believed it; she did not know that, condemned to be subject to the yoke of a superior force, a woman cannot escape her destiny, and that everything around her, even temporary successes, was preparing the chains of slavery for her weakness. We wisps of straw, slaves of an invisible power, blindly obey the fatality that guides us. It was that fatality, the ruler of the world, which had placed Cymodora's secret in my hands—and I would see her again!

Filled with that hope, I returned to the place to which my heart summoned me. My expectation was not mistaken. I heard Cymodora coming. She was searching anxiously for the *pensées* abandoned to the breezes of the shore. I followed all her movements. In haste to give rise in her soul to a new emotion, I began to play a lyre strung in the Lydian fashion, and enjoyed her surprise.

Oh, how disconcerted she is by the unfamiliar sound of a voluptuous harmony! How charming it is to see her trembling with agitation, her ears attentive, her hands reaching out, scarcely breathing for fear of disturbing the sonorous air that carries my chords around her!

Her charming attitude reveals both the desire to listen to me and the dread of being seen. She tries briefly to resist the impression she is experiencing. Vain effort! Her disturbance carries her away. She cannot help being seduced. Her light footfalls skim the ground. She comes nearer, to listen at closer range. I hear her; I see her. Suddenly, the tune ceases, and I appear.

"Daughter of Greece," I say to her, "don't be afraid. I am not seeking to trouble your innocence, to ravish your liberty. No, I swear it, and you may believe in a stranger who admires you, a voice that begs you; I only want to enjoy the delight of hearing from your mouth the story of the misfortunes of your fatherland, and will withdraw thereafter if you tell me to do so. Born to command, I shall be your slave. Speak, and I will obey."

This manner of speech, new to her, dissipated her fear. She looked at me with astonishment. Her emotion was visible.

"Stranger," she said, "tell me by what enchantment you produce sounds so pure and so touching. Your art is dangerous. It is full of charm, but harmony ought to awaken courage and not enervate by means of the intoxicating softness of its chords. Don't you know that, in the great days of Athens, a Greek was pursued for having invented a seventh string for the lyre."

"Yes," I replied, "but when Timotheus was led to the public square in order to be subjected to his sentence, he perceived that the statue of Apollo was holding a lyre similar to his own in its hand. At this unexpected protection, he uttered a cry, showed the people the instrument that had served as a model, and prostrated himself—and his judges dared not condemn an invention consecrated by the attributes of a god."[22]

---

[22] Cymodora and Nadoor Ali appear to be misquoting this story. Timotheus of Miletus (446 BC-357 BC) was an innovative musician who added extra strings (probably four in number) to the *cithera* [lyre], which had previously had seven

My reply surprised Cymodora. She blushed, remained silent for a moment, then said: "I must admit that the virile pride of your manner, the gentleness of your speech and everything about you inspires a confidence in me that I had thought impossible. But what is your intention? What hope bought you to this desolate shore? Have you come to contemplate our superb temples, admire the ancient monuments to the glory of the Greeks? You will see that they are no more.

"No vestige remains of those famous Areopagi, and that tribunal of harangues in which the thunderous eloquence of Demosthenes roared, and the elegant chariot of Alcibiades made the dust fly in the arena of the Olympic Games. Like the devastating fires that devour everything they find in their path, the barbarians have passed over the soil of Athens, and ancient Athens has disappeared. They have ravaged our fertile fields, shaken our porticoes, profaned the tombs of heroes, delivered the inspirations of genius to the flames and smashed the statues of our gods. Like the unworthy sailor gripped by fear at the approach of a tempest, degenerate Greece has fled before the impiety of those people who are enemies of gods and humans alike.

"Personally, to escape their fury, I hide my wandering life from their sacrileges. Raised in the ruins of a Christian church, founded long ago by a French prince, on the most obscure pint of one of our river-banks,

---

strings. It is said that when he visited Sparta, the outraged citizens seized his *cithera*, removed the extra strings and hung the mutilated instrument up in the public square to shame him, in spite of his protest that a statue of Apollo in the same square depicted the god's *cithera* with the same number of strings as his own.

adopted by the savant Alcidamas, a virtuous priest who educated my youth in the religious sentiments of our forefathers and the hatred of slavery, I lived with him, in the woods, far from mortals who are ever oppressive and mendacious. Alas, Alcidamas is dead. The gods have closed his eyelids, made heavy by age. My eyes watched him expire, bathed with tears. My hands hollowed out the ground that received him.

"As I speak to you about that generous friend, though, I don't know what fear takes hold of my senses. I imagine that I can still hear his dying voice. He is saying to me: *Cymodora, flee from men and you will be free.* I swore an oath to do so on his icy lips. O Father! I shall hold to that terrible oath. I shall be pure and free like you, and my soul, which disdains the weakness of slaves, and is aroused by the mere thought of a generous action, conserves the energy that you were able to inspire within it."

Thus spoke Cymodora, and her animated speech had a magic, a splendor and a majesty that tended toward divinity. I was in an ecstasy impossible to describe. I could not weary of seeing and hearing her.

Surprised by my long silence, she stared at me. What a gaze she had! It embraced my heart. My disturbance increased. I could not help myself; my knees bent; I fell at her feet. She blushed and, rising angrily to her feet, tried to leave.

"O Cymodora!" I said. "Forgive me—I could not resist the ascendancy that your beauty and the expression over your voice have over me. Can the abandonment in which you leave me inspire fear? It's you who have given rise to the intoxication that possesses me, it's for you alone that I have felt the love that you condemn and which might itself condemn you, when it is you that it

147

inspires. If you forbid Nadoor Ali, an admirer of the heroes of your fatherland, who has known battle himself, to raise his voice toward you, at least accept the aid of his arm. War might desolate these climes again, brigands infest these shores. Fear them. In the name of Alcidamas, whose memory you have invoked, in the name of the very gods you serve, O Cymodora, permit me to protect you against the perils that surround you."

"Protect me!" she said. "Have I not my long-proven arrows? Woe to those who brave them!"

"Leave this place, where your liberty is under threat."

"I am free!" she cried, proudly."

I saw then that time alone could dispose her reason to understand the as-yet-unknown dangers.

"Well," I said to her, "dispel your fears. Yield to my plea; stay; tell me about the misfortunes of Alcidamas, and explain by what remarkable circumstance an elegant daughter of Athens has become a solitary virgin of the woods."

"Tomorrow," she said. "Dusk is approaching. The horizon is veiled, the night darkening. I have to go away. Farewell!"

With these words, she escaped. Less impatient in her accustomed course, however, she slowed her pace, turned her eyes toward me, resumed her progress, reached the top of the hill, stopped, looked at me again, and finally fled the place that she might soon never see again.

What diverse impressions are produced by the departure of a beloved woman! What memories her absence recalls simultaneously to our confused senses! At the moment when she leaves us, it seems that our soul follows her and leaves with her. The foliage that shaded

148

her head, the place that she occupied, the flower that ornamented her hair, the pleats of her floating tunic, the
stone that her hand has touched, the places where she has
walked, even the air that she has breathed, everything is
filled by her image, everything seems to repeat the farewell that she pronounced.

Tomorrow, Cymodora had said. She had said that!
She hated and shunned men, but my presence had ceased
to irritate her. I had spoken to her; she had listened; she
had permitted me...what am I saying? She had *ordered*
me to see her again.

Tomorrow!

I would see her, I would be close to her, I would enjoy her gaze, I would be intoxicated by her smile, and
perhaps then, a thousand times repeated by the lover
who adored her, a tender confession, a word, a single
word long retained on her charming lips, might finally
escape involuntarily....

3

The next day, the heat in Athens was scorching. I
waited impatiently for the evening breeze to refresh the
air, and ran to the place I thought I would reach before
Cymodora. But how can I describe my despair when,
having reached the shore, I saw a boat ploughing
through the waters, and Cymodora, already captive,
reach out to me with arms laden with odious chains, to
appeal for futile aid?

I recognized the kidnappers. They were mercenary
pirates who reap, over the immensity of the seas, the
gold of Asian harems. I displayed to their eyes a sign
revered in our climes: a dagger glittering with precious
stones, an indication of my elevated rank, but my terrible

voice carried the cries of my impotent rage to them in vain. Their vile souls, closed to all human sentiment, open to the sole avidity of riches. Those brigands, pitiless devastators of coasts, were insensible to the repeated outbursts of my distress as they fled, and soon I could no longer see either the boat or Cymodora.

There are cruel situations in life whose bitterness one cannot describe. A terrible dart that breaks he heart exhaust our combines forces in the experience, and leaves none for its expression. The fate of Cymodora absorbed my thoughts entirely.

"I shall never see her again!" I cried. "What has become of that superb daughter of Athens, so proud of her liberty? A slave beneath a foreign sky, she will no longer tread the protective soil of her homeland. She will die far from the tomb of her forefathers."

Cymodora had delighted me. I no longer had any hope of seeing her again. I conceived a horror of he places that she had fled forever, and searching everywhere for a vessel to take me away, I embarked at Corinth and set out for Benares.

I made the journey rapidly. The news of my return soon spread in Benares, and when I appeared, the atmosphere resounded with the pompous noise of instruments and the joyous cries of an immense crowd that covered the banks of the Ganges.

The Rajah came to meet me in person. Azolida accompanied him. Carried by slaves in a rich palanquin, she stopped on the bank, and when she lifted her veil, I was dazzled by her beauty and the emotion that animated her features. I knelt down; she reached out to me with a hand I felt trembling in mine, and forced me to sit beside her.

The homage rendered to me resembled the honors of a triumph. It was with that brilliant procession, preceded by bayaderes performing graceful dance-steps, surrounded by my guards and Indians who were calling me their liberator, that we arrived at the palace. There, everything was laid out for a fête. A sumptuous banquet was ready.

The Rajah invited me to sit next to Azolida, and said to me, in the presence of his entire court: "Nadoor Ali, learn the reason that caused me to hasten your return. Azolida was unable to bear your absence. Her grief awoke my compassion. She confessed her love for you. I owe you a recompense worthy of me and the services that you have rendered my people, who love you, and I have chosen you to be the support and heir to my throne. Tomorrow, you shall be married to my beloved daughter."

The running gazelle struck by the hunter's arrow, the warrior struck by a mortal blow, the errant voyager struck down on the desert sand by the inevitable blast of lightning, are not more shocked than I was by that unexpected news. Azolida fixed upon me eyes filled with the softest hope, and seemed to be waiting for my response.

I realized the necessity. I collected myself and, forcing myself to smile, I bowed my head before the Rajah as a testament of my gratitude—but my heart, occupied by a love foreign to that which was offered to me in flattering homage, shivered involuntarily at the unhappiness that I undoubtedly foresaw.

Soon, the signal for music was given. The Rajah, yielding to the keenest joy, said: "Friends! Sing the exploits of Nadoor Ali!"

Scarcely had my name been pronounced than a scream emerged from the midst of the harem slaves, who were still some distance away. It seemed to me to be a bad omen. I was nonplussed. Azolida blushed and went paled by turns, and her anxiety as extreme. But then all the pleasures of the Orient surrounded us, perfumes rose up, the songs began, and my disturbance escaped everyone's eyes in the tumult of varied dances and brilliant chords that filled the palace.

Eventually, the Rajah ordered everyone to be silent, and asked me to tell the story of my voyage. I obeyed. I gave rapid descriptions of the various countries that I had visited since my departure from Benares: the enchanting landscapes of Switzerland; the glory and talents honored in the fortunate fields of France; the fine arts admired in Italy and the ruins of superb Athens. With what charm I recalled the places, so dear, that I had recently quit.

Carried away by a sudden inspiration, my heart stirring and my features taking on a more animated expression, my voice became louder as I talked about the famous heroes of Greece, the monuments raised by genius on the soil of Attica and, finally, the harmony of the chords heard on the shore of the Aegean Sea.

The Rajah listened to me with flattering attention. He was moved, and when I had finished speaking, he shouted "Selim! Have the new captive brought forward."

In response to his order, a young slave came forward, took the lyre, and struck a chord.

Her veil fell.

Gods! It was Cymodora!

The Pursuit of Lord Ruthwen
(continued)

VIII

Nadoor Ali is interrupted. Someone is knocking forcefully on the door of the house in which the three friends have taken refuge. It is opened. An envoy from Duc Albini comes in mysteriously, introduces himself and explains the subject of his message thus:

"I have orders to take you to the palace via a secret door. the governor is waiting for you."

"What does he want?"

"I don't know."

"Where shall we see the minister?"

"At the fête that is being held this evening at court. You will be there. That's all that I can tell you. Let's make haste to leave."

At that moment, dawn is beginning to break.

Nadoor Ali, Aubrey and Léonti follow their guide, who recommends the most extreme prudence to them, and, by a roundabout route, they soon reach the Duke of Modena's palace.

Part Three
The Duke of Modena's Minister

I

Alfonso II, Duke of Ferrara, who died childless in 1597, declared Cesare d'Este to be his universal heir in his will. The new duke expected to be crowned by Pope Clement VIII, but the court of Rome, for the most frivolous of reasons, claimed that the Duchy of Ferrara devolved to the Holy See. Far from recognizing Cesare as the legitimate successor of Alfonso II, the pontiff published a decree by which he declared him incapable of succeeding to the Duchy of Ferrara, excommunicated the prince, along with anyone who helped him to maintain himself there, and submitted the city to a prohibition.[23]

---

[23] Save for a couple of mistakes that probably originated as typos (which I have corrected), this basic account is accurate. Alfonso d'Este (1553-1597) became Alfonso II, Duke of Ferrara, in 1559, after which he became an important patron of the arts and sciences, playing host to Torquato Tasso, among many others. When he died childless, the Holy Roman Emperor, Rudolf II, recognized his illegitimate cousin Cesare d'Este as Duke, but lacked the will to provide material support when Clement VIII (born Ippolito Aldobrandini) decided to annex the city of Ferrara to the Papal States, with the result that the papal army met no opposition. Cesare d'Este then moved his court to Modena, where his early years were troubled by disputes between the Ferraran lords who accompanied him and their Modenese counterparts. The rest of the story is, however, entirely fictitious; Cesare had married Virginia de Medici in

Papal troops, numbering 25,000 men, approached the Ferrarans. Duke Cesare, unable to obtain the help of any other power, decided to solicit an ecclesiastical order, and asked for a truce.

A clever man was required to conduct that important negotiation. The Duke entrusted it to an English nobleman who had captured his entire confidence. A statesman and profound politician, adorned with a brilliant exterior and that suppleness of mind which determines success at court, Lord Seymour had arrived in Ferrara a short time before, and had become the friend and confidant of the prince. He immediately accepted an embassy that opened a door to his ambition.

Cardinal Aldobrandini, the pope's nephew and legate to Bologna, was transported to Faenza, the place chosen for meetings. Thanks to his skill, the Duke's minister obtained a capitulation, specifying that Cesare would be absolved of all censures on renouncing the possession of the Duchy of Ferrara and its dependencies, and ceding to the Pope half the artillery and arms that were in the city.

The Duke left Ferrara and went to establish his court in Modena. He devoted his cares to the embellishment of his new capital, and made it much more brilliant than the city he had abandoned to the pretensions of the Roman court. In a short while, Ferrara was depopulated and deserted.

Lord Seymour was appointed as the Duke of Modena's prime minister. At first, that nascent court had all

---

1586, but none of the five daughters she bore him—in spite of recurrent fits of madness—was named Eleonora; the eldest was Giulia (born 1588). Although history is rich in Ducs d'Albini, none seems to have been attached to Cesare's court.

the hopes that a new government usually entertains, but the loved of novelty, light as it is, cannot resist the friction of rival parties. Partisan spirit, blunted, denatured and lost under a strong government, reawakens, grows and extends under a weak prince. In politics, the worst of systems is not to have one. An uncertain progress, which lowers tomorrow those it raised up yesterday, has all the physiognomy of perfidy, and perfidy leads to disorder.

Such was soon the situation of the Duke of Modena's government. The Ferrarans, who had left their forefathers' fields, wanted account to be taken of their voluntary emigration, while the Modenese bitterly criticized the desire of foreigners who aspired to all favor.

The prince abandoned the reins of state to his prime minister, who was accused of an irresistible penchant for evil. More than once he was seen to protect vice at the expense of virtue, to stifle the voice of justice, the cry of pity and the voice of honor. From then on, a discontent that became more extensive every day, might have led to great public calamity, but in those happy times fidelity recoiled from the abyss of revolution.

Duc Albini, the former minister of the Duke of Ferrara, was the governor of the palace of Modena, and his son was in command of the guard. Numerous services and an utterly proven devotion had given the respectable old man the right to voice the truth, whose language is all too often misunderstood in the courts of princes. He had seen, painfully, a stranger take possession of an authority that should have been his. Accustomed to unveil the intrigues of cunning politics, he anticipated that the new favorite would have a stormy administration, and sometimes warned the Duke of misfortunes that he feared—but his courageous voice was unheeded.

In the palaces of kings, virtue often appears criminal, while the perfidious language of flattery corrupts everything around it, conspires, triumphs and narcotizes the prudence of the monarch with regard to the dangers that the present is preparing for the future.

Meanwhile, Lord Seymour, having reached the summit of honors and power, saw everyone bend to his law. The severity of his gaze and the deleterious modification of his features appeared to be the effect of his application to public affairs, but in the fêtes held in the palace he showed so much readiness in his intelligence and so much grace in his language that all the women of the court were desirous of his attentions.

The Duke had only one daughter, whom he cherished. In accordance with his orders, gatherings were held in the princess's apartments, where witty and varied conversations embellished the leisure of fine evenings. On such occasions, everyone would offer a true or imaginary account of some recent amorous adventure, or some ingenious tale whose moral was always applauded when it was amusing.

One evening, when there was talk of witchcraft and of a vampire that had caused the death of a young woman in Florence, Lord Seymour, pressed in his turn to pay his tribute to the assembly, yielded gracefully to the princess's desire. The courtiers gathered around him. Everyone was listening attentively.

He began:

"It is well-known that all peoples have their prejudices and their superstitions. Some are bizarre. Such is the superstition of the *evil eye*, of whose influence the Sicilians have a singular dread. The evil eye, it is said, acts suddenly; it causes a sudden malady; it fills the imagination with lugubrious visions; it removes the means of continuing projects begun. The same superstition exists in Scotland; it existed among the ancient Greeks and is conserved by their modern descendants. I read in a Greek book this strange passage:

"*I do not call the evil eye a superstition, but a certain venomous faculty of reason. I have personally witnessed several effects of the evil eye, in particular, one day when I chanced to find myself with one of these fascinators, whose eyes afflicted several children and, that same evening, a vine. I asked him many questions, but all that he told me was that during the fascination he felt a certain acridity and warmth in his eyes, and a impulsive desire toward the object.*

"*I wanted to see an experiment, and I asked that some handsome and well-nourished animal should be brought to us. A young water-buffalo, well-fattened and quite beautiful, was indeed brought to us. As soon as the sorcerer had glimpsed it, he asked me whether I wanted him to strike it with his gaze. 'Yes,' I said, 'I would like that very much.' And, as he fixed his eyes on the buffalo, it immediately collapsed, as if dying, foaming at the mouth and grinding its teeth. He quickly ran forward and touched the poor beast three times with his right hand. It was not long delayed in getting up, and was returned to the herd.'*

"The most bizarre thing about this anecdote is that it is recounted by one of the most learned men in Greece.

"In France where everything seems to be reproduced with the lightness and chivalric grace that has made the powerful nation in question the most amiable and most admired of peoples, pleasing fables and established prejudices are distinguished by a piquant mixture of seriousness and gaiety. Tales of witches and revenants are no exception.

"There are also various superstitions in Spain handed down through the centuries. Some reflect the character of that religious people, and others were imported by the Moors when, drawn far from their native lands by the spirit of conquest, they invaded the kingdom of Grenada.

"The Orientals, especially, mingle superstitions with all the activities of life. In addition to the admission of fatalism, they have created god and evil genies, vampirism is undoubtedly another dream of their imagination extrapolated to extraordinary conceptions.

"There has been much talk for some time of a vampire who travels through all countries, leaving victims in his wake everywhere. Ignorance has accredited this news, and all women tremble when they encounter a vagabond traveler whom fear has made into a redoubtable monster.

"I will certainly not deny the existence of vampires; I have even seen, in a few periods of my life, misfortunes that might have caused me to believe in them. I think, however, that the horrible crime that signals vampirism is more an allegory, the moral of which has several applications—for example, a conqueror who ravages peaceful countries, and whose insatiable ambition sheds the blood of peoples; an ingrate and prodigal son who reduces to poverty a virtuous father whose sixty years of labor had assured his fortune; a woman one loves and who, by virtue of her imprudence, continually sharpens the dagger of jealousy for us; a cruel king; a perfidious friend; a minister who betrays the confidence of his master and brings about a terrible revolution instead of the wellbeing that he could have produced. Do not all these individuals, the scourges of society, represent vampir-ism?

"Indeed, if one could always part the clouds with which the inexplicable cruelties of men that are called vampires are surrounded, one would often see that the fear they inspire is only produced by misfortunes beyond the scope of our intelligence, or by misapprehensions that, once clarified, make us blush at our credulity. That idea reminds me of an oriental story that fortifies my opinion. Here it is:

The Vampire of Baghdad
An Oriental Tale

1

Not far from Baghdad, the superb city built by the Caliph Abu Jafar Al-Mansur, which served from then on as the residence of the masters of the Orient, in a hut on the edge of a little wood, lived a poor fisherman named Gia Hassan. The tools of his trade and a few reed mats woven by his daughter Phaloa were all he possessed. The Tigris, whose waters flowed a short distance away, furnished them with sufficient for their nourishment and their needs.

Every day, after the morning's fishing, Phaloa went to the city to sell the fish caught in her father's nets and the baskets rounded by her pretty fingers. It did not take Phaloa long to place her provisions. She was so pretty that the merchants came running to crowd around her, and she soon came back, singing, to deposit the proceeds of the daily sale and the evening's work in Gia Hassan's hands—who gave her a paternal kiss. A simple and frugal meal, and the evening prayer, terminated these peaceful occupations. Thus it was that, poor but honest, unknown but tranquil, Gia Hassan and Phaloa passed days without remorse or regrets, which might have been envied by the Commander of the Faithful.

In that era, the great and redoubtable Haroun al Rashid reigned in the Orient, a Caliph powerful not only by virtue of the force of his arms, which he had caused to be respected beyond his realm, but also by a combination of the rarest and most fortunate qualities, which had earned him the love of his people. Full of grandeur and generosity, Haroun did not entrust the duty of rendering his people happy to his ministers alone. He listened personally to their slightest protests, judged their disputes by making the interested parties appear before him—and, more than once, when justice gave him a duty to pass sentence on an unfortunate, the latter would go away laden with the Caliph's consolations, bearing a double indemnity for the loss that he had just suffered.

Peace had recently terminated a war provoked by the ambition of one of the provincial governors submissive to the Caliph. Haroun had covered himself in glory, re-established order and punished the guilty parties. His return to Bagdad excited a universal joy. His subjects welcomed him not as a king but as a father. The Caliph, moved by their rapture, felt more than ever the happiness of being loved—the sole recompense and sole pleasure that sovereigns ought to be ambitious to attain.

Among the soldiers who formed the Caliph's guard there was one named Khaled. This young man, long employed in a corps retained in a distant location, was recalled when peace was declared. The honorable advancement he received proved that his good conduct had been appreciated, but as his tastes inclined him toward trade, in which estate his parents had brought him up, he waited for a favorable opportunity to indulge that penchant and obtain from his commanders the initial provision necessary to his plans—liberty.

While walking outside the palace one day, Khaled saw a young woman pass by whose grace, attractiveness and—most of all—air of modesty, struck him to the point of disturbance.

"O Divine Prophet," he cried, "If the houris that you promise to true believers have as much feminine charm as that young beauty, what felicities you have reserved for them!"

And Khaled, in saying these swords, followed the young woman, who, as fresh as a morning rose and as nimble as a Lebanese kid, was hastening to reach the bazaar, doubtless to dispose of the burden she was carrying in her arms.

As she neared the end of her journey, the young woman stumbled, and was about to fall—but Khaled, who was following close on her heels, was fortunate enough to catch her in his arms. Several baskets full of fish slipped from her hands. A merchant to whom she was accustomed to sell her wares recognized her immediately and ran to her, saying: "Beautiful Phaloa, how often have I pitied you for not having the help of a brother or a friend! May our Holy Prophet send you a model husband, in order to reward your virtues."

Frightened by the prospect of falling, Phaloa has not paid any attention at first to the stranger who helped her, but now she looks at him, and her face is overtaken by a vivid red blush. The stranger is beside her; it is he who protected her from danger, and yet he seems to be trembling more than her. He has heard the sound of Phaloa's touching voice, and all the sensations he experiences are combined into one desire: to love her and be united with her forever.

With her eyes lowered, the daughter of Gia Hassan addresses timid thanks to the unknown who is proclaiming his devotion and his delicacy, and does not want to suffer her to return home alone. He takes the merchant as a witness to his honest intentions, and adds: "I am Khaled, soldier of the Caliph. May God grant that I never sully with the slightest stain an irreproachable conduct esteemed by all my commanders. I shall escort this young woman, and return her safe and sound to her father's arms."

Phaloa has already received the price of her merchandise. Khaled, on whose arm she is leaning, blushingly, has already passed through the city gate. A few more minutes and they are on the plain, no longer able to hear anything but the distant muffled rumor of the noise of Bagdhad, the cadenced roar of the waves of the Tigris nearby on their right, and the harmonious songs of the birds of the evening all around them—a thousand various cries resounding in the air.

Oh, how their love was stimulated! How deeply the imposing spectacle of nature—a spectacle of love and pleasure in those fortunate climes—plunged their souls into a soft languor! There were not saying anything, and only looking at one another clandestinely, but it seemed to them that the magical scene had a language known to sensitive souls, which no two individuals could interpret in a different manner.

They were still absorbed in these pleasant thoughts when the sight of her father's hut struck Phaloa's gaze. She thought she was emerging from a dream. Entirely given to the new sensation that had overwhelmed her, she was not singing the customary song as she approached the refuge of happiness. The old man seemed troubled on seeing his daughter with a stranger. He was quickly reassured by Khaled, who provided the necessary clarifications, but could not help allowing the ardor that he felt and the hope he dared to entertain to show through his discourse.

2

Khaled was endowed with a pleasant physiognomy. His regular features expressed gentleness. He had lived in military camps, but his virtue, which was not alarmed by pleasure, had a horror of licentiousness. His heart was pure, and when he spoke, the accent of truth seemed to emerge from his lips. He soon gained the confidence of Gia Hassan and the affection of his daughter. He returned more than once to visit the fisherman, but Phaloa, who always felt renewed pleasure on seeing him, did not perceive that he had become necessary to her existence had her happiness.

One morning, Khaled came at the time for fishing. That was not his habit; a somber sadness transformed his facial features. His pallor and depression threatened bad news. Phaloa shivered without knowing why; her hear froze with fear. Gia Hassan ran back as quickly as he could in response to his daughter's voice, and Khaled, a little calmer but not reassured, spoke to them in these terms:

"Worthy Hassan and charming Phaloa, you know what the dream of my happiness is. You know how attached to you I am, and my love for Phaloa is no longer a mystery. What you do not know is that, having resolved to make her my wife and certain of his consent, I asked my commanders for the honorable discharge that my services merited, and permission to take my bride to the Mosque.

"Nadir, the officer of the Caliph, under whose orders I still am, had promised me that. The days passed, however, and my situation remained the same. A secret presentiment caused me to be very fearful of that slowness.

"O fatal difficulty, deadly thought! It has been realized only too soon. Yesterday, when I returned to barracks, distressing news was spreading. War has broken out again, with greater fury than before, and the Caliph, who has had ample time to rest and enjoy all the pleasures with his numerous mistresses, is making preparations to depart.

"O Phaloa! O Hassan! I have to go with him, to leave you...perhaps to perish far from here, far from you and the beauty that has become my happiness!"

As he finished speaking, his voice died on his lips and his head slumped forward on to his breast. He was unable to weep, but the precipitate movement of his sighs and the languor of his gaze testified to the dolorous disturbance by which he was tormented.

The old man and Phaloa made no reply. Hassan's daughter thought she was dreaming, but waking up seemed so difficult that she dared not move for fear of acquiring a frightful certainty.

Eventually, she emerges from her stupor. It's really him...it's Khaled...he's going away...

At this idea, her heart breaks, and her beautiful eyes moisten with tears.

"Daughter," says the fisherman, "don't abandon yourself to sighs. Perhaps everything is not as desperate as you believe. The Caliph is not insensitive. I intend to take you to him tomorrow. We shall embrace his knees, and ask him for brave Khaled's liberty—and if the sight of my white hair cannot persuade his clemency, your youth, beauty and tears will obtain the beneficence of his noble and generous heart."

Thus spoke Hassan. The souls of the two lovers, like a sea whose waves are agitated and broken against the rocks by a furious storm, seemed suddenly to calm down, as if by magic. Smile reappeared on their lips, and soon, along with the smiles, a soft radiance of hope colored their cheeks.

Animated by this sweet hope, Khaled set forth along the road to Baghdad, where his service was required. The two lovers swore once again a fidelity proof against anything.

The old fisherman, who had no need to seek information about Khaled to judge his good qualities, smiled at the sight of the young lovers' innocent intoxication. He blessed them privately. They would be the support and consolation of his old age. They were his entire future—and an old man's future is so brief! Gia Hassan made Khaled promise to come back and share their modest evening meal.

Phaloa did not go to the city that day. Her lover's absence caused her distress. What if the Caliph were inexorable? What if he disdained a poor fisherman's prayer? She was beginning to feel that, although love has its sweetness, it is mingled with exceedingly cruel pain.

While absorbed in these reflections, Hassan's daughter, without being aware of it, went toward her lover.

She was alone in the middle of the plain when a stranger enveloped in a large cloak approached and, with an expression that radiated generosity, said to her: "Young woman, you're weeping. Who, then, could sadden such beautiful eyes? In the name of Mohammed, may the traitor who has caused your tears to flow perish!"

"My lord," the timid Phaloa replied, "the Caliph is the sole cause of my grief."

"The Caliph!"

"In person."

"By what hazard?"

Then, ingenuously, Phaloa tells the stranger the story of her love, her hope, and the bad news that has just destroyed it. She talks about the poverty and virtue of her father, the bravery and services of Khaled, and, finally, the plan that they have made to go and throw themselves at the feet of the Commander of the Faithful the following day.

The unknown man, touched by her candor, admits the interest that she had inspired in him. He picks up a brick that happens to be lying on the ground, and draws a portrait on it.

"Take this drawing, beautiful Phaloa," he says, "and when you go to the palace, be sure to show it. I am an officer of the Caliph, and I will make every effort to persuade him to show favor to your desires."

After saying this, he follows the young woman to the fisherman's hut. Phaloa introduces the unknown man to her father as her liberator. The old man hastens to invite him to share a modest meal. The officer accepts, eats and drinks with a hearty appetite, and intones a few verses from the Qur'an. Soon afterwards he rises to his feet.

"I regret being obliged to leave you so soon," he says, "but the hour is nigh when service summons me to the presence of the prince. Farewell, my dear friends; farewell, charming Phaloa—don't forget what I told you. Remember, furthermore, the name of Nadir."

As he concludes this speech the stranger is on the threshold of the hut; he squeezes Phaloa's trembling hand, and disappears.

Scarcely has he gone when Khaled comes into the hut; he has met the stranger, who hid his face. Khaled loves Phaloa passionately, and is certain that he is beloved, but, being young, ardent and impetuous he cannot help feeling a twinge of jealousy. His anxiety and his precipitate questions give him away. He seems to be contemplating a plan that he wants to hide. When Phaloa tells him about the affectionate interest that the unknown man has manifested toward her—the portrait on the brick, the supper, the tender manner in which he squeezed her hand, it is all reported with the simplicity of innocence. Then the young man asks whether the sympathetic individual deigned to give his name.

"My son," says Gia Hassan, "his name is Nadir."

"Nadir?"

"Yes, Nadir—an officer in the Caliph's guard."

"He's an impostor, a knave, a traitor. Nadir is my commander, and I've just this moment left him. O charming Phaloa, I suspected as much; your charms have seduced this stranger, whose bearing is not unfamiliar to me. I even recall…yes, I'm certain now of having seen him several times roaming the streets of Baghdad at dusk, and on the banks of the Tigris. He's a dangerous individual, I no longer have any doubt about that. Dread his perfidious designs. Do you know what this infamous seducer is capable of doing? Do you know what dangers his ominous presence can cause? Know that he is a vampire."

"A vampire!" says Gia Hassan.

"A vampire!" the fearful Phaloa repeats, pressing herself against her father.

"Yes, a vampire. He's one of those monsters that have long been the terror of this region, and whose victims so many young lovers and unfortunate relatives have had to mourn. Alas, I only required this misfortune to reduce me to despair."

The worthy old man and his daughter tried to dispel the alarm that had arisen in Khaled's agitated heart, but the young man, as impatient as all lovers are, informed them of a new subject of distress. The Caliph could not be seen the following day. The privy council had to discuss important measures required by the war. It would not be possible for them to get into the palace until the day after, and a day's delay might bring significant events.

Phaloa dismissed all these obstacles and, by means of a reasoning that was frail, but which desire succeeded in making seem sufficient, succeeded in restoring hope to her lover's heart. It seemed to her, whether because a secret voice promised her that her charms would win the Caliph's consent, or because an optimistic presentiment told her that her lover's fears were exaggerated, that she was very close to the moment of happiness.

Women have a kind of prescience and rapidity of judgment that serves them admirably, and hazard often leads them to that which they desire or that which they have foreseen.

3

The following day, but earlier than on the previous day, the stranger returned to the hut. Phaloa, who as alone at the time, could not suppress a fearful movement.

"What's the matter, beautiful Phaloa? Who can be causing you such dread?"

"Oh, My Lord, if one can believe what is said, you're an exceedingly terrible man."

"Exceedingly terrible in what way?"

"A monster."

"A monster? Who could have given you such flattering information about me?"

"Khaled."

"Khaled?"

"Yes, My Lord; he says that you're a vampire."

"Me, a vampire! What does he mean, a vampire?" And the stranger suppressed a surge of anger that almost escaped him. "Can you believe, charming Phaloa, that I mean you any harm? My eyes don't say so, though."

"Men are very perfidious."

"Oh well—go see the Caliph; you'll soon know how far my perfidy extends. I'll have my revenge on Khaled...but... Farewell!" Having said that, he disappears, as on the previous day.

Phaloa begins to tremble; the unknown man had terrible eyes when he pronounced Khaled's name.

Gia Hassan returns. Phaloa makes him party to her fears—and this time, they are well-founded. Oh, how slowly the day seems to go by.

Finally, dusk arrives. Khaled presents himself at the door of the hut, but scarcely has he set foot within it when guards, who were hidden nearby, fall upon him, take him captive and disarm him. Frightened by their sudden appearance, Gia Hassan and Phaloa utter futile screams. They throw themselves at the soldiers' feet. They are told that it is on the Caliph's orders that Khaled has been arrested. The bewildered young man asks what his crime is, but no one can tell him anything, except that he is to be taken to the palace prison.

At these words, the unhappy Phaloa falls unconscious. The poor fisherman covers her with tears and kisses. The unfortunate Khaled, whom the soldiers lead away in spite his resistance, has lost all hope of happiness.

The next day there was a public audience at the palace. Caliph Haroun al Rashid, surrounded by his senior officers and seated on a throne whose splendor dazzles the sight, rendered justice in person and listened to the claims of his subjects.

Khaled in brought before him, free but disarmed. His distressed face testifies to his despair. He lowers his eyes, prostrates himself and waits in silence for someone to deign to interrogate him. A murmur of sympathy rises up around him, but he is deaf. He does not turn his head to look at the crowd, or the young beauty beside him covered by a veil sparkling with gems, who is looking at him tenderly. One sole thought preoccupies him, which is Phaloa's anxiety, and even the presence of the Caliph cannot distract him from it.

Immediately, a voice makes itself heard. "What harm has the Caliph done to you for you to have dared proffer insults against his sacred person? Answer, Khaled!"

"My service beside the Commander of the Faithful, and that blood I have shed in is cause, answer for my fidelity to his person. My tongue has never been able to belie my heart. I swear as much by Mohammed!"

"You boast of your services; for some time, however, you have solicited the favor of being set free."

"I adore the charming Phaloa, the daughter of Gia Hassan the fisherman. I can only live for her. I thought that my brave arm had paid its debt to my master, and that I might live or myself now."

"A short while ago, you brought a serious accusation against an unknown man."

"A stranger introduced himself to my beloved. I was suspicious of him, and suspect him of harboring evil intentions. I admit that I believed that he was a vampire, and said so."

"Raise your eyes, and behold that vampire."

Heaven! The Caliph! Amazing!

Khaled falls to his knees.

"Get up," says Haroun al Rashid. "Receive a thousand purses for your good conduct, be free, and marry Phaloa."

At these words, Khaled turns his head, and the young woman takes off her veil. O joy! It is Phaloa herself! She is accompanied by her father. She falls into her lover's arms. All three prostrate themselves, moved by gratitude to the Caliph, and the sympathetic people manifest in applause the pleasure they experience in seeing justice and love triumph.

The Duke of Modena's Minister
(continued)

II

When the minister had ceased speaking, everyone gave evidence of what a pleasure it had been to hear him—the Duke by means of a flattering word, the courtiers by means of praise, the ladies by means of soft gazes, and he princess by means of a smile.

Thus, Lord Seymour's credit increased further every day, and he already seemed to be at the pinnacle of his desire, when an unfortunate event—but a favorable one from his viewpoint—gave him even more entitlement to the complete confidence of the prince.

Princess Eleonora has hosted a concert in her apartments that the entire court has attended. It is late; the singing has ended, the harp is no longer resounding, people are leaving and already, all is calm.

Everyone is asleep, but thick smoke, gradually increasing, has disturbed the Duke's sleep. The air that he breathes brings a weight with it that oppresses his breast. He sits up, calls out, drags himself out of bed, staggers and falls into the arms of a devoted subject who races to snatch him from the jaws of death—just in time.

A terrible blaze is revealed; a hidden fire explodes violently; the flames increase, devouring everything they can reach. The alarm bell chills everyone with fear; the fear increases the tumult; the burning doors collapse noisily, and smoking debris soon marks the place where the superb palace stood.

The Duke wanted to know who his rescuer was. It was his minister, Lord Seymour himself. He did not know how show his gratitude for a devotion that other people interpreted differently. He led him by the hand to his daughter, and said to her as he presented him to her: "This is the man who saved my life; it is for you to judge the reward he deserves, and to pay your father's debt."

Left alone with Lord Seymour, the princess, disconcerted by the price's final words, stammered a few thanks, and then added: "The memory of such a service will always be dear to me, but the expression of my gratitude ought to be sufficient for you. What reward could a minister at the height of his power desire?"

"There is one far above the honors of the court."

"What?"

"It depends on you."

"On me?"

"My assiduous attentions, my respect, my haste to please you, to talk to you, and my silence when I am near you, ought to have informed you what it is."

"My Lord!"

"Perhaps you forbid desires too unworthy of you. Forgive me—I saved your father's life, and to save yours, I ran…"

"What! It was you who snatched me from certain death in the midst of the chaos of frightful darkness?"

"What are you saying, Princess? Who snatched you from death, when, how and where? Go on."

"The fire had made rapid progress. Isine and Placida, my faithful companions, had run in search of help. Frightened by the danger that surrounded me I had almost lost the use of my senses, and believed myself lost forever to the affection of a father, when I felt myself being carried away by an officer, who withdrew rapidly after returning me to the arms of my friends."

"Who was this officer?"

"I don't know—the darkness did not permit me to recognize him."

"Can no clue allow you to identify him?"

"The plume from his helmet remained at my feet. It proves that he's an officer in the palace guard. That's all I know."

"Well, Madame, we must find out. Duc Albini's son commands the palace guard; he'll be summoned, and he'll help us in our search. The man who risked his life for you cannot be honored too highly. Let the most splendid favors be the price of a peril for which I would have given my life. The Venetians have declared war on us; the army is under my orders; let us give its command to a warrior who was able to deserve it by saving the life of the Princess of Modena. Here's the order; you shall convey it to Albini. Your rescuer must receive it in your name. If the power that I hold on your father's behalf has precious advantages, it is at this moment that I appreciate them most of all."

This gesture of generosity on the minister's part was inspired more by the desire to get rid of a dangerous rival that his amorous desire feared than by a sentiment of justice and benevolence. Eleonora was deceived by it, and her heart was softened by it.

It was then that young Albini appeared. A black armband veiled his armor, and all his features were impregnated by a faint melancholy.

"Princess," he said, "I've received an order to present myself before you. Deign to tell me what the object is of such a great favor."

"My Lord," said Eleonora, "Before anything else, permit me to ask you why your arms are covered by funereal attire."

"Madame," Albini replied, with embarrassment, "Don't seek to penetrate a mystery that I cannot reveal to you. The mourning that surrounds me is dear to me, and I've sworn to wear it until the day I recover my lost plume."

"Your lost plume. Wait—it can be replaced by another. I want you to take it from my hand."

"What! Madame…"

"Here it is."

"Heavens above!"

"Do you recognize it?"

"Madame," said Albini, embarrassed. "No…I can't…"

"No!" Eleonora repeated, with a sigh. "To whom does it belong, then?"

"Perhaps, one day, you shall know."

"Albini," said the minister, interrupting, "that officer is under your command; it is up to you to discover him. The army is waiting for him; let him show himself worthy of the honor that the princess has solicited for him."

"You see, Albini," Eleronora added. "This is his reward—that he leaves."

"If you order it, he will leave."

"I'll keep his plume; I want to give it back to him myself."

Such generous gestures are all the more dangerous for being filled with charm.

"I shall pray for the success of his arms and for him."

"And for him!" cried Albini, enraptured. "Farewell then, Madame, farewell! He will die for you, or he will return victorious."

Before the end of the day, the princess learned that Albini had departed for the army. Was it, therefore, him who had saved her life? But for what motive had he made a mystery of his devotion? His anxiety in speaking to Eleonora, and perhaps the dread of explaining himself in front of a dangerous witness, gave rise to the suspicion of his love for the princess—and his silence, which proved his delicacy, gave an even higher value to the sentiments that he had not dared to declare.

Eleonora, in the flower of youth, shone with the beauty that brings with it an irresistible seduction. Her slender, elegantly-proportioned figure outlined, as if by magic, forms that were the perfection of nature. Her features were dazzling in their expression and vivacity. Nothing was ever more expressive than her gaze, more delightful than her smile, daintier than her delicate feet. Art would have searched in vain for faults in the piquant mixture of so many various qualities; everything was graceful. The charmed eye saw nothing but her. In sum, her entire person was an enchantment, and if she was not beauty itself, it was because she was a hundred times more beautiful.

The princess was absorbed in reveries of which Albini was the object when the Duke presented himself in her apartments and expressed the desire to see that she shared the love of the minister whose wife she was to be. A father's will was a command to her; not knowing how to reply, she promised to obey. The minister, enchanted by her consent, gave the most lavish fêtes to please her; he was amiable, and he succeeded in interesting Eleonora. Their marriage was decided.

Meanwhile, Albini lost no time in demonstrating his courage. Every day the court learned of the success of the army under his orders. For political reasons that no one could understand, however, far from rewarding the service of its officers, the favors refused to them were lavished on sedition-mongers, and the minister gave his support to the prince's enemies. The palace governor, an old friend of the Duke, sought in vain to diminish his credit. The Duke only saw through the eyes of his favorite, to whom he had granted his daughter.

The marriage was to take place the following day. A brilliant fête was in preparation, a hunting meet was arranged, to begin the pleasures.

III

They set forth; a numerous cortege follows the princess. They separate in the nearby forest. The horses support the ardor of the hunters; the heat is excessive. The princess draws away from her followers and pauses in a shady spot. There, solitary and pensive, she yields to memories that she had tried in vain to forget. A secret anxiety is pursuing her. In a few hours she will plight her troth to Lord Seymour. She does not experience any repugnance with regard to forming that bond, and yet a more tender sentiment causes her to regret the generous Albini.

Her mind is drifting in this fashion when a stranger appears before her.

"Lovely princess," he says to her, "I have come here to save your life. Fear the knot that you are about to tie; the day of your marriage will be that of your death. The husband you have chosen is a monster, and your life will be lost in his first embraces. This language astonishes you; alas, it is all too true. You see in me one of his victims; time will inform you of others. Don't neglect my advice, and flee the misfortune that is about to overtake you."

Troubled by what she has just heard, Eleonora tries to call the stranger back, but she has scarcely recovered from the stupor that the mysterious messenger's speech has occasioned when the entire court arrives in her vicinity. They surround her. Lord Seymour presents her with her charger. The signal for departure is given, and they resume the road to the palace.

After a sumptuous banquet, the dancing begins. A thousand varied games embellish the fête. The princess, tormented by the fears that she cannot dispel, avoids the homage of the courtiers, and beneath a disguise that favors her desire to hide herself from all eyes, she searches everywhere for distractions that flee before her.

Suddenly, a masked individual stops her, and says to her: "Listen, O most adorable of women! It's in vain that an impenetrable veil hides you from every gaze. Mine has followed, divined and recognized you. By that noble bearing, the grace that animates all your movements, and that enchanting lightness of foot, who could mistake the beautiful Eleonora?

"Forgive a lover who adores you a confession that might cost him his life. In your presence, his heart have not dared to declare itself, but his voice will make itself heard. A pure love like that you inspire, delightful as it is, might have betrayed itself before you, but it has kept silent, and it requires all the mystery with which it envelops itself at this moment to abandon itself to the pleasure of speaking to you. O Eleonora…!"

At these swords, the irritated princess snatches away the unknown man's mask. A cry goes up within the assembly. It is Albini!

"Young man," says the Duke, with a severe expression, "Why have you left the army without my order?"

"My Lord," says Albini, "I have often risked my life in battle for you. My courage, attested by glorious exploits, gives me the right to my prince's confidence, and I have left my soldiers in order to render you a more important service. I know that someone has poisoned your mind against me. I know my enemy, but, less anxious to defend myself against his blows than to enlighten you as to the misfortunes that threaten your own person, I have come to accuse explicitly the minister who is betraying you."

"Who, then are you accusing?" says he prince.

"Lord Seymour," replies Albini. "Yes, it is the minister himself that I accuse here, and you shall shortly hear the witnesses of his crimes."

At the same instant, a curtain opens, which reveals the stage on which the musicians and singers are placed, and Aubrey, Léonti and Nadoor Ali appear, disguised as troubadours.

Aubrey

All smile in delight at the lute of the troubadour,
Tender ballads expressing tender amour,
The so-called sickness devoid of cure.
Beside the object that makes his heart adore.
Happy, he sings of pain that makes his heart soar
Unhappy, he sings all the more.

Léonti

But our weary voices can no longer resound,
For happiness; what song can be found,
When the heart by love's uncrowned.
When love has fled, upon the hallowed ground
On which on hear its last farewell unwound,
The final dream of life is drowned.

Nadoor Ali

Beloved palm-trees, my homeland's blue skies!
Burning sand whose storms sting my eyes,
Cymodora before me flies.
In the desert where she heard my cries,
She is no more, alas, all beauty dies
To avenge her, I will arise.

All Together

Prince! Subjects! All of you pay us heed.

Rich, honored, you are the victims of greed.

It seeks in vain its lust to feed.

The king of the weak hears the wretched plead.

The vengeful cry of mortal virtue freed

Demands that the guilty should bleed!

"Stop!" says Lord Seymour. "Insolent adventurers, introduced into the palace to import disturbance and slander!"

"I recognize him," says Aubrey, forcefully. "Lord Seymour is Lord Ruthwen; he's the one who killed my sister!"

"It's him!" says Léonti. "He's the one who stole my dear Bettina from me."

"Yes," adds Nadoor Ali, "he's the one who left Cymodora lifeless in the deserts of Arabia."[24]

"He is also the one," another voice continues, "who gave the secret order to set fire to the prince's palace in order to promote his ambition with a reputation for devotion without running any risk."

"Beware of the vampire!" they all cry, vehemently.

Fear and astonishment are painted on every face; everyone awaits the outcome of such an extraordinary scene. The prince seems anxious and irresolute, and al-

---

[24] This is inconsistent with what Nadoor Ali told Aubrey and Léonti before he began telling them the (conspicuously unfinished) tale of his relationship with Cymodora, when he said that she was a prisoner in Arabia—but it is, of course, necessary to the symmetry of the narrative that Ruthwen/Seymour should have killed her

ready it is evident that, giving little credence to what he has just heard, he wants to listen to his prime minister's justification. He orders that the fête should continue and that the gates of the palace should be locked, and then withdraws to his study. Lord Seymour follows him, and such is the force of the ascendancy he has obtained over the prince that a few moments suffice for him to lead him astray again and persuade him to do everything he wishes.

Soon, the news spreads that the governor of the palace has been exiled, Aubrey, Léonti and Nadoor Ali arrested.

From that moment on, Albini senses that he will be sacrificed to the minister's vengeance. Surprised to be still at liberty, he follows a crowd of courtiers gripped by fear, fleeing in all directions. He does not notice that someone close to him is moving at a precipitate pace. He has already reached the palace gates when, just as he is about to go through, guards that had long served under his command block his passage, surround him and press upon him.

"Our worthy leader," they say to him in a whisper, "our companion in arms, our benefactor, old warriors that love you offer you their lives. Our arms are ready."

"Against whom?"

"Against your enemies."

"My enemies are those of the prince whom we serve. It is in battle that warriors like you ought to show their courage."

"Your life is threatened. Our recognition desires to save you."

"My honor is opposed to it."

"We are supposed to capture you."

"Obey, then."

"The minister has ordered it."

"And I forbid it," says the princess, forcefully, removing her mask. "Palace guards! Recognize my voice."

"Madame, it's what you wanted. I have no complaint regarding my fate."

"Cruel! The step I'm taking at this moment tells you what a mistake I've made. Time is pressing, Albini. Flee! It's me who is imploring you."

"Guards! Do your duty."

"Our duty is to avenge you. Speak—who is the victim it's necessary to strike?"

"Me! I have given you an example of valor; I must give you one of fidelity. The order bears the prince's seal; obey, I tell you."

"We embrace your knees. At least yield to our prayers, our tears."

"Ah!" says Albini, moved. "Get up. I order you to, friends, I beg you to do so. The prince has spoken, here are my weapons. Let's go."

"So the voice of Eleonora has no effect on the heart of Albini!"

"Eleonora!" He pauses, looks at the princess, then says as he draws away: "Farewell, Madame; I feel that it is sweet to die by your hand."

"He loves me, he sees my pain and he blames me!" says the princess, sobbing. "Alas, irritated by a declaration that offended me, I thought to punish the audacity of a lover unworthy of me, and it's Albini that I've doomed—Albini, who is dear to me, to whom I owe my life. Well, it's now up to me to save him. Yes, I shall save it, even at the expense of my own."

So saying, she runs to lock herself in her apartments. A thousand plans whirl through her mind, conceived one moment and destroyed the next. Finally, she settles on the hope of changing her father's mind. The night has gone by and sleep has not closed her eyelids. Pale and distressed, her eyes still swollen with tears, she presents herself at the Duke's door and asks to see him in private.

Introduced into his presence, she says: "Father, the commander of your guard, the leader of your army, the warrior so faithful in the service of his prince, who vanquishes the enemies of his fatherland and whose glory has given splendor to yours, Albini, arrested at the gate of a palace he defended for so long, has been treated as a vile criminal. I have come to demand justice."

"Daughter, why do you take such a great interest in a guilty man."

"Guilty? He is not."

"He has left the army."

"In order to give you important information."

"He has slandered my minister."

"He has been deceived."

"He dares to love you; he told you so."

"That was when my hand tore away his mask."

"The motive that directed your action accuses you."

"It justifies me. If I had known that it was him, I would have respected his secret."

"It's true, then that you share his insane love, and that, dishonoring your father and yourself, you have received Albini by night in this palace? His plume was found in your apartments."

"O Heaven! What outrage is being done to me? And you can tolerate it?"

"Your enthusiasm to defend him is sufficient proof that he is guilty, and will pay with his head…"

"Stop, Father—know my innocence and Albini's generosity. He is the one who saved my life when fire broke out in the palace; in the disorder inseparable from the peril to which he exposed himself, he dropped his plume, which I kept in order that I would one day know my savior and lead him to your feet. My Lord, deign to have Albini brought before you; interrogate him yourself. You will know everything; you will render him justice. Oh, Father, be not deaf to your daughter's prayers and the voice of truth. I embrace your knees; you are softening, I can see…I hope. I will run to fetch the proof of Albini's devotion."

She leaves precipitately, arrives at her apartments, demands and searches for the desired plume—but in vain.

IV

At that moment, someone comes to inform the princess that a tribunal convened by the minister will pass judgment on her savior. Gripped by fear, she remembers her father's reproaches. The plume can no longer be found—how suspicious! Who, then, has dared to take possession of it? Only one man, a party to the secret, and impelled by jealousy, is capable of making it serve his vengeful plans. She is, however, resolved to try anything to confound that odious imposture.

Indignation gives her energy, and she is already making preparations to appear in person at the tribunal when the minister appears, and tells her that Albini has been condemned to death.

"That sentence is unjust," said Eleonora. "He will not be executed. I shall go, I shall speak, I shall defend him, and my father will hear me."

"Abandon that hope. Your father has approved Albini's condemnation."

"Cruel! It's you who have arranged everything. You have too much power in the court, but you'll answer to me for Albini's life. You must set aside this odious sentence."

"What you ask of me is beyond my power."

"Enable him to flee, then; sign the order to set him free this instant, or fear my despair."

"If I betray my duty in order in order to refuse you nothing, will you refrain from giving the man any hope that you love him?"

"What are you demanding of me?"

"That you yield to the desires of your father, who wants me to receive your hand at the altar this very day, without delay."

"Sign, then—I'll consent to anything."

"If that is your wish."

"Give it to me."

"Remember your promise. You'll be mine."

"I swear it."

"Well, Princess, you shall have to obey. Here's the order you desire. This evening, at midnight, in the palace chapel."

Thus, everything cedes to the politics of the cunning Ruthwen. He orders and directs the preparation for his wedding. The entire palace is at his sole disposal, and his master has only the shadow of supreme authority.

There is, however, a noticeable anxiety in the Duke's mind that bodes ill for his minister. He seems to be avoiding him, listening to him with embarrassment and following his advice mistrustfully. With a single word, he could break the yoke whose danger he did not foresee—but he does not have the strength to pronounce that word.

Since the condemnation of Albini, he has locked himself in his study, invisible to everyone except Lord Ruthwen, whom he no longer loves, but still fears.

Such is the fate of a prince who abandons the reins of state to a favorite. He bemoans the misfortunes that offend his generosity, but which his weakness authorizes. Severe with his most faithful friends, he is indulgent to those who are betraying him.

While everything presages an imminent catastrophe in the palace, Albini, shackled in irons, awaits the fateful moment that will reveal his scaffold. He had appeared before his judges fearlessly. Proud of his innocence and the services he had rendered to the state, he was impatient to justify himself—but when, after being reproached for his desertion of the army, he was shown his plume as evidence of his criminal attempts on the Princess of Modena, surprised by the unexpected attack, he thought that Eleonora had taken sides against him. That idea made such a profound impression on his consciousness that he refused to defend himself.

Now condemned, and without hope, his prison resounds to a single groan.

"Is Eleonora my enemy, then?" he said. She too furnishes evidence to have me condemned! And great God, what evidence! That which recalls everything I have done for her.

"Ah, mortal thought! This is the reward for my devotion. The pain has broken my heart, and yet that heart loves her still, alas! It will only cease to beat for her when I cease to breathe.

"But while I mourn her, the ingrate is perhaps in the midst of pleasures...what sobbing can I hear? Who is coming towards me?

"Oh you, unknown creature, who alone has pity on my misfortune, what do you want of me? Why have you come to this frightful abode?

"You sigh, you press against me, you bathe me with your tears—speak; who are you?"

"Can't you recognize me?"

"Heavens! Eleonora!"

"I've come to break your shackles."

"You! Here! Now!"

"Oh, you don't know what your liberty has cost me."

"Explain yourself, celestial creature."

"I have made a terrible, horrible sacrifice for you, because I love you, because I adore you."

"What do you mean?"

"Know that, as the price of the order I've obtained to snatch you from the scaffold, I must marry…"

"Who?"

"Your enemy."

"Great God!"

"I've promised."

"No—that frightful marriage shall not take place. Think what will become of your life."

"I'm only thinking of saving yours. Follow me. I desire it; I command it; obey, or I shall die at your feet."

"Very well, yes, I'll go with you. A new hope is gleaming in my troubled mind. It inspires me; it inflames me. It's the one hope that remains to me. Yes, adored woman, angel of heaven, I shall save you once more, and I'm hastening to do so."

"What is your plan?"

"Go back to the palace. Tomorrow, at daybreak, we shall be avenged. Farewell!"

The Princess cannot hold him back; she fears that the fury that animates him might lead him to his doom. A terrible silence reigns around her.

As she ran to her lover's prison she had but one sentiment, one idea; she forgot all the dangers. Now that he is free, she is alone; through the shadows of the night she steers an uncertain course, passing through deserted areas.

She wanders through the darkness in this way for some time.

V

Finally, confused and trembling, Eleonora reaches the palace. They are waiting for her; the ceremony is already prepared. Her late appearance is criticized. Her friends dress her against her will. Soon, led to the redoubtable chapel, pallor on her brow and her heart broken, she puts on the nuptial headband, the fatal headband, symbol of imminent death.

The Duke observes her despondency, and is alarmed. The minister attributes it to a transient illness, impatient for the moment that will render him the happiest of men.

Eleonora yields to her father's order, and her mouth allows a consent to escape that, scarcely pronounced, becomes irrevocable. One instant more, and the beautiful Eleonora, Albini's generous friend, will see her life extinguished on the marital bed where happiness out to await her.

The following day, however, the greatest disorder reigns in the palace. The Duke is told that his daughter is expiring; the tolling of the church bell brings the faithful hurrying from all parts.

Public prayers begin, but they are interrupted by a general murmur. A woman launches herself on to the steps of the altar.

It is Bettina.

"People," she says, "listen to me. Last night I presented myself at the palace to warn the unfortunate Eleonora about the fate that menaced her. My voice was lost in the air, and an unknown hand suddenly struck me with a poisoned dart. A vampire is my assassin, and that of the Princess of Modena. It is the minister of your prince; your prayers for his daughter are futile. Eleonora is dying. Avenge me; avenge her."

Having said that, she falls, rolls on the sacred floor, and dies in horrible convulsions. Then the church doors are flung open, and a company of armed men runs in.

Léonti flies toward Lord Ruthwen, plunges a blade into his breast, and immediately withdraws it, dripping blood, in order to strike himself with it.

The tumult is at its height. A cry of vengeance rises up on all side. Albini shows himself, harangues the people, lays his weapons down at the feet of the prince and sears to defend him. His warriors do likewise, and in accordance with his advice, they run to the palace to render life to the Princess.

There was no longer time.

With her last breath, Eleonora pronounced Albini's name.

The mourning of such a great loss was increased day by day by further anguish. The most beautiful ladies of the court were dying, without any detectable cause. Edolinda, the flower of Italia beauty, Countess Azelina, the lovely Zerbina and the tender Petrilia were perishing of an unknown sickness.

After a thousand vain conjectures, memories were consulted. Aubrey awoke just suspicions against his enemy.

The genius of evil never dies for its crimes, and such is the horrible privilege of a vampire—but how could those tenebrous mysteries be penetrated? How could they be resolved? What could be done?

Eventually, they run to the place where the infamous Ruthwen's corpse has been deposited. The earth is dug up, the grave opened.

O surprise! A hideous pallor covers the face of the odious cadaver, but by a miraculous contrast, it offers bloody vestiges of life.

Its sparkling eyes shine with a terrible expression, launching darts of fire, and its bloodied red lips are moving, writhing, seemingly still feasting on a frightful meal.

At the sight of this phenomenon, the witnesses recoil in horror; the envoys of the court, forced the recognize the truth of an event beyond all belief, write the irrevocable proof of it on a piece of paper that will conserve the story in the annals of Modena.

The prince is informed and immediately orders that, in order to prevent further calamities, red hot irons should burst the eyes and traverse the heart of the monster.

After this execution, death ceases its ravages. The Duke is inconsolable for the loss of his daughter and so many misfortunes.

Albini heaps benefits on Aubrey and Nadoor Ali and persuades them, without difficulty, to settle in Modena with him.

Appointed as prime minister, he deploys every effort of his genius and zeal to heal the state's wound, but such is the frightful abyss left behind by the rapid transit of an evil minister that a long period of care and sacrifice scarcely suffices to restore order and peace in the Duchy of Modena.

Finally, Eleonora's generous rescuer did the same for the state; by sage but energetic measures he stifled the spirit of revolt and civil discord that then infested Italy—and history, which stigmatizes perfidious custodians of power and advertises virtue and fidelity to future generations, has transmitted in permanence, to the gratitude of the people of Modena, the honored name of Albini.

The end of Lord Ruthwen

A Manuscript Discovered

Lord Ruthwen did not imagine that his end was so near when he went to the church with the Duke of Modena; he had not taken any precautions. After his death, his apartments were searched, and beneath a marble slab cleverly set against a wall and hidden in an obscure alcove, a little iron box was found, securely locked. It was necessary to break it to open it. This mysterious strongbox contained a manuscript, which bore the singular title: *The Story of My Early Life*

This manuscript was deposited, in that already distant era, in the ducal library, and stolen by a Venetian during the Italian wars. The same family conserved it for several generations in archives abandoned to time and dust, and it finally became the property of as French artist who, learning of the publication of *Lord Ruthwen*, has just offered us this text. This is how it fell into his hands.

In 1797, on a winter evening, having returned to his lodgings to work on the views of Venice that he had been sketching for several hours in a gondola placed in the midst of the lagoons, he asked for a fire. In order to light it a servant brought a heap of old papers, among which were the story of Lord Ruthwen's early life. That title piqued his curiosity. He hastened to start reading it, and the events recounted in the curious history interested him so keenly that he took care put the bizarre manuscript away in his portfolio. We might perhaps be able to publish it, if we are encouraged to do so by some success.

Notes on Vampires

The singularities of Lord Byron, in his private life, have contributed no less than the originality of his talent to make him famous in England. Overtaken while still young by a black melancholy, sharpened by domestic misfortunes and unjust slanders, he renounced his fatherland and, wandering from one country to another, might have been thought to have become a stranger to the human species.

Independent by virtue of his fortune as well as his genius, he only wrote by virtue of inspiration, and, untroubled by criticism and praise, disdained the rules of art and the conventions of society alike. By a bizarre preference, he chose for his heroes men who set themselves above all laws and sacrificed all the rights of humanity to their pride. It was a new road that he wanted to follow.

In his bold compositions he loved to paint in dark colors everything that struck his imagination, and the virile energy that characterized his Muse sometimes degenerated into harshness. Through the darkened scenes in which he seemed to delight, however, he drew from his Muse details full of grace and freshness, which proved his talent for descriptive poetry.

Among the number of his depictions remarkable in that fashion, we shall only cite a single passage from *The Corsair*. When Medora describes for Conrad the anxieties of his absence, the story of what she has experienced while separated from him has, in the original version, an inexpressible charm. We have tried to translate the passage as follows:[25]

> Oh! Many a night on this lone couch reclin'd,
> My dreaming fear with storms hath wing'd the
> [wind,
> And deem'd the breath that faintly fann'd thy sail—
> The murmuring prelude of the ruder gale....

Lord Byron's works remarkable in that, combining poetic merit with the interest of prose romance, they are based on extraordinary adventures that, having sharply piqued curiosity, leave the ultimate fates of their heroes uncertain. They thus create an exaggerated desire for a denouement, which, in seeking to divine it, the imagination augments at will. This method, which is not exempt from reproaches, is very piquant and perhaps best fulfils the aims that are bound to propose themselves to an author who does not disdain to combine the inspirations of a poet with the less elevated schemes of a novelist.

---

[25] I have only quoted four lines from Byron's text (beginning with line 369) whereas Bérard's "attempted translation" has eighteen. There seems little point in quoting eighteen because Bérard's version bears very little resemblance to the original; although it seems evident enough which passage he means, his version does not even qualify as an accurate paraphrase. Having tried to retain the rhyme and approximate scansion of some of Bérard's poetry, I am well aware of the necessities of improvisation involved translating verse from one language to another, but it seems to me that he is being deliberately disingenuous in naming his poem as a translation rather than an independent piece inspired by Byron's. I cannot see any point, however, in my attempting a back-translation of his verse into English.

Whatever place Lord Byron ought to occupy in English literature, however, our intention is not to address that question but to expand further on the beauties and faults of his works.

The Vampire is, without a doubt, the most extraordinary of all Lord Byron's compositions. It is well within the compass of his ideas, but his style is not recognizable therein. It is one of those mental aberrations that genius dares not admit. It is said that Lord Byron, pressed by his companions to tell a story in his turn, improvised the adventures of a vampire which have since been collected and delivered to print by his friend, the physician Polydory.[26] The work in question bears none of the imprint of Lord Byron's talent. The story is bizarre and frightening, and that is doubtless what has secured its success. It is the extraordinary vogue that the romance has inspired that gave birth to the project of supplementing it with the sequel that we are now publishing.

We shall not seek to explain here the folly of the superstition of vampirism. That incredible disorder of the imagination of ignorant peoples is probably merely the result of an as-yet-unknown malady. The authors of dictionaries define a vampire thus: "A man dead for several months or years who returns, becomes visible, walks, talks, and drinks the blood of the living."

---

[26] Just as the actual title of the work Bérard is discussing is, of course, spelled with a *y* rather than an *i*, and its author's name with two *i*s rather than two *y*s. If this alteration is deliberate, its motive is presumably similar to the one that led to the substitution of Ruthven by Ruthwen, but the probability is that Bérard was dictating to an amanuensis unfamiliar with the name.

Notes

Addenda to Part Two

The adventure of Antonio came from Saint-Remy, a pretty little town in Provence renowned for its Roman antiquities and a lunatic asylum. That madhouse is in a delightful valley in the foothills of the Alps. Gardens maintained with extreme care, abundant springs of an admirable purity, a keen and excellent atmosphere that renders the wind buffeting the rocks more salubrious and enchanting beauty spots embellished by the beautiful southern sky all combine to form a perfect setting for a place that serves as a refuge for unfortunates lost to society.

Monsieur Mercurin, the famous physician,[27] devotes his varied talents to the prosperity of that fine establishment, which is inhabited by the insane of many lands, and to which even this country has sometimes paid tribute.

Independently of the pharmaceutical aid lavished on these unfortunates deprived of reason, however, two powerful resources collaborate in the numerous successes that obtain the physician's well-deserved reputa-

---

[27] This is presumably the physician Louis-Étienne Mercurin whose marriage was registered in Saint-Remy in 1788, but he was neither the first nor the last physician with that surname resident in the town. The Louis Mercurin who donated an organ to the local church in 1845 might have been the same person, but was more probably his son.

tion: music and the meeting of the two sexes, for two hours every day, under the surveillance of the servants attached to the house. It is impossible to describe the impatience of these unfortunates while they await the moment that will bring them together in the vast concert-hall. Several of them are musicians; they sing; the orchestra accompanies them, and they applaud he pleasure they experience themselves.

An even more curious spectacle, however, is to see them dancing after the concert. They choose their partners for the quadrille or the waltz. A perfect decency reigns in these meetings, at which, to the joyous sound of drums, all the pretty Provençal girls throw themselves collectively, who form quadrilles indiscriminately with the inmates of the house or the young swains that accompany them. A meek joy shines on every face and, amid that pleasant tumult, which presents the most bizarre contrasts, it is difficult to recognize the unfortunates who are mad in the midst of those who pass for sane.

The madman who, in order to escape from his retreat, employed the extravagant means that we related in the story of Antonio, is still alive. His name is Renaud. Except for his madness—and perhaps because of it—he is said to be the most amiable, the most cheerful and the wittiest of the creatures that one might find in such an abode, where the absence of reason more frequently offers travelers the distressing spectacle of human degradation. It is also Monsieur Mercurin's establishment that inspired a few scenes of the story of the young Moravian woman.

We should not conclude this note about Saint-Remy without pointing out an essential error into which several otherwise-praiseworthy writers fall. It is a league from that small town that the ancient court of love presided over by the Abbess de Sade and the beautiful Laure is located. In the woods of Romarin one can still see the ruins of the château where that amorous court held its sessions. We do not know why Madame de Genlis, in her new novel *Pétrarque et Laure*, and the estimable author of *La Gaule poétique*, have placed the court of love near Avignon.[28] That monument to chivalric times

---

[28] There are several peculiarities in this passage, not the least of which is the reference to the "*Abbesse de Sade*" [Abbess de Sade]. The background to the reference is that the uncle of the infamous Marquis Donatien de Sade, Jacques-François de Sade (who was an Abbé [a priest without a parish]), wrote a biography of the Italian poet Francesco Petrarch, who spent his early life in exile living in the Sades' native Provence. He subsequently recalled catching a glimpse of a girl named Laure leaving a convent near Avignon on April 6, 1327, which became a lifelong obsession and the inspiration of all his work. The Abbé de Sade argued (convincingly enough to have the allegation reproduced as fact in most subsequent reference books, even though Petrarch's claim might well be pure fiction, inspired by Dante's account of his fateful glimpse of Beatrice) that the girl in question must have been Laure de Noves, who subsequently married his ancestor Hugues de Sade. Donatien de Sade recorded his own inspirational vision of Laure, experienced in a dream after reading his uncle's text while in prison.

The book by the Comtesse de Genlis to which Bérard refers was published in 1819; it is not a *roman* [novel], although it is not an orthodox work of literary criticism either. *La Gaule poétique* was an oft-reprinted showcase anthology by Louis-Antoine de Marchangy, first published in 1813. The literary fame of the ruined château to which Bérard refers was subsequently renewed by a poem by the Provençal poet Frédéric Mistral, "Romarin," which in turn inspired a notable short

is curious enough in itself and in the memories it recalls for its true location to be fixed with exactitude.

The White Woman is a ghost story accredited in a few villages in Normandy. We heard the story of that apparition told at a pleasant gathering at the house of the Comtesse de B***. The remainder is invention, and we have transposed the setting to Naples.

In Rome, as in all the lands of the south, the heat is so intense during the day that dusk is awaited with impatience. Then, like errant shades in the Elysian Fields, men and women walk abroad, while other breathe in the coolness of the evening at the doors of their houses. Singing and the music of guitars are heard everywhere, and if one combines that magical scene with the varied effects of the moon, whose white light filters through the trees, one will have an idea of all the pleasure that such a spectacle inspires.

It is from the piquant work of an Arab poet that we have borrowed the idea of a young female vampire.

---

story by Jean Lorrain, "L'Âme des ruines" (tr. as "The Spirit of the Ruins").

Addenda to Part Three

Political, literary and religious almanacs have furnished us with the historical narrative of the Duchy of Modena, and a scholarly article in the *Journal des Débats*, which appeared in 1812 the curious details of the superstition of the *evil eye*.

The manner of death that we have chosen for our vampire in the denouement is described in *Les Préjugés de tous les peuples*, a work by M. Salgues.[29]

End of the Notes

---

[29] The actual title of this work by Jacques-Barthélemy Salgues is *Des Erreurs et des préjugés répandus dans les dix-huitiène et des dix-neuvième siècles* [Errors and Preconceived Ideas Widespread in the Eighteenth and Nineteenth Centuries] (1811).

SF & FANTASY

Xavier Mauméjean. *The League of Heroes*
John-Antoine Nau. *Enemy Force*
Marie Nizet. *Captain Vampire*
C. Nodier, A. Beraud & Toussaint-Merle. *Frankenstein*
Henri de Parville. *An Inhabitant of the Planet Mars*
J. Polidori, C. Nodier, E. Scribe. *Lord Ruthven the Vampire*
P.-A. Ponson du Terrail. *The Vampire and the Devil's Son*
Maurice Renard. *The Blue Peril; Doctor Lerne; The Doctored Man;*
A Man Among the Microbes; The Master of Light
Albert Robida. *The Adventures of Saturnin Farandoul; The Clock of*
the Centuries; Chalet in the Sky
J.-H. Rosny Aîné. *Helgvor of the Blue River; The Givreuse Enigma;*
The Mysterious Force; The Navigators of Space; Vamireh; The
World of the Variants; The Young Vampire
Han Ryner. *The Superhumans*
Brian Stableford. *The New Faust at the Tragicomique;The Empire of*
the Necromancers (The Shadow of Frankenstein; Frankenstein and
the Vampire Countess; Frankenstein in London); Sherlock Holmes &
The Vampires of Eternity; The Stones of Camelot; The Wayward
Muse. (anthologist) *The Germans on Venus; News from the Moon;*
The Supreme Progress
Jacques Spitz. *The Eye of Purgatory*
Kurt Steiner. *Ortog*
Eugène Thébault. *Radio-Terror*
Villiers de l'Isle-Adam. *The Scaffold; The Vampire Soul*
Philippe Ward. *Artahe*
Philippe Ward & Sylvie Miller. *The Song of Montségur*

MYSTERIES & THRILLERS
M. Allain & P. Souvestre. *The Daughter of Fantômas*
A. Anicet-Bourgeois, Lucien Dabril. *Rocambole*
A. Bisson & G. Livet. *Nick Carter vs. Fantômas*
V. Darlay & H. de Gorsse. *Lupin vs. Holmes: The Stage Play*
Paul Féval. *Gentlemen of the Night; John Devil; The Black Coats*
('Salem Street; The Invisible Weapon; The Parisian Jungle; The
Companions of the Treasure; Heart of Steel; The Cadet Gang)
Emile Gaboriau. *Monsieur Lecoq*
Steve Leadley. *Sherlock Holmes: The Circle of Blood*
Maurice Leblanc. *Arsène Lupin vs. Countess Cagliostro; Lupin vs.*
Holmes (The Blonde Phantom; The Hollow Needle)

Gaston Leroux. *Chéri-Bibi; The Phantom of the Opera; Rouletabille & the Mystery of the Yellow Room*
William Patrick Maynard. *The Terror of Fu Manchu*
Frank J. Morlock. *Sherlock Holmes: The Grand Horizontals*
P. de Wattyne & Y. Walter. *Sherlock Holmes vs. Fantômas*
David White. *Fantômas in America*

SCREENPLAYS

Mike Baron. *The Iron Triangle*
Emma Bull & Will Shetterly. *Nightspeeder; War for the Oaks*
Gerry Conway & Roy Thomas. *Doc Dynamo*
Steve Englehart. *Majorca*
James Hudnall. *The Devastator*
Jean-Marc & Randy Lofficier. *Royal Flush*
J.-M. & R. Lofficier & Marc Agapit. *Despair*
Andrew Paquette. *Peripheral Vision*
R. Thomas, J. Hendler & L. Sprague de Camp. *Rivers of Time*

NON-FICTION

Stephen R. Bissette. *Blur 1-5; Green Mountain Cinema 1; Teen Angels & New Mutants*
Win Scott Eckert. *Crossovers* (2 vols.)
Jean-Marc & Randy Lofficier. *Shadowmen* (2 vols.)
Randy Lofficier. *Over Here*

HEXAGON COMICS

Franco Frescura & Luciano Bernasconi. *Wampus*
Franco Frescura & Giorgio Trevisan. *CLASH*
L. Bernasconi, J.-M. Lofficier & Juan Roncagliolo Berger. *Phenix*
Claude Legrand, J.-M. Lofficier & L. Bernasconi. *Kabur*
Franco Oneta. *Zembla*
L. Buffolente, Lofficier & J.-J. Dzialowski. *Strangers: Homicron*
Danilo Grossi. *Strangers: Jaydee*
Claude Legrand & Luciano Bernasconi. *Strangers: Starlock*

ART BOOKS

Jean-Pierre Normand. *Science Fiction Illustrations*
Raven Okeefe. *Raven's L'il Critters*
Randy Lofficier & Raven OKeefe. *If Your Possum Go Daylight...*
Daniele Serra. *Illusions*

CPSIA information can be obtained
at www.ICGtesting.com
Printed in the USA
LVHW031123191221
706634LV00002B/325

9 781612 270043